THE SAUGATUCK CONSPIRACY

THE SAUGATUCK CONSPIRACY

DAVID OSBORN

DAGMAR MIURA

LOS ANGELES

Published by Dagmar Miura
Los Angeles
www.dagmarmiura.com

The Saugatuck Conspiracy

First published 2023

ISBN: 979-8-89195-000-9

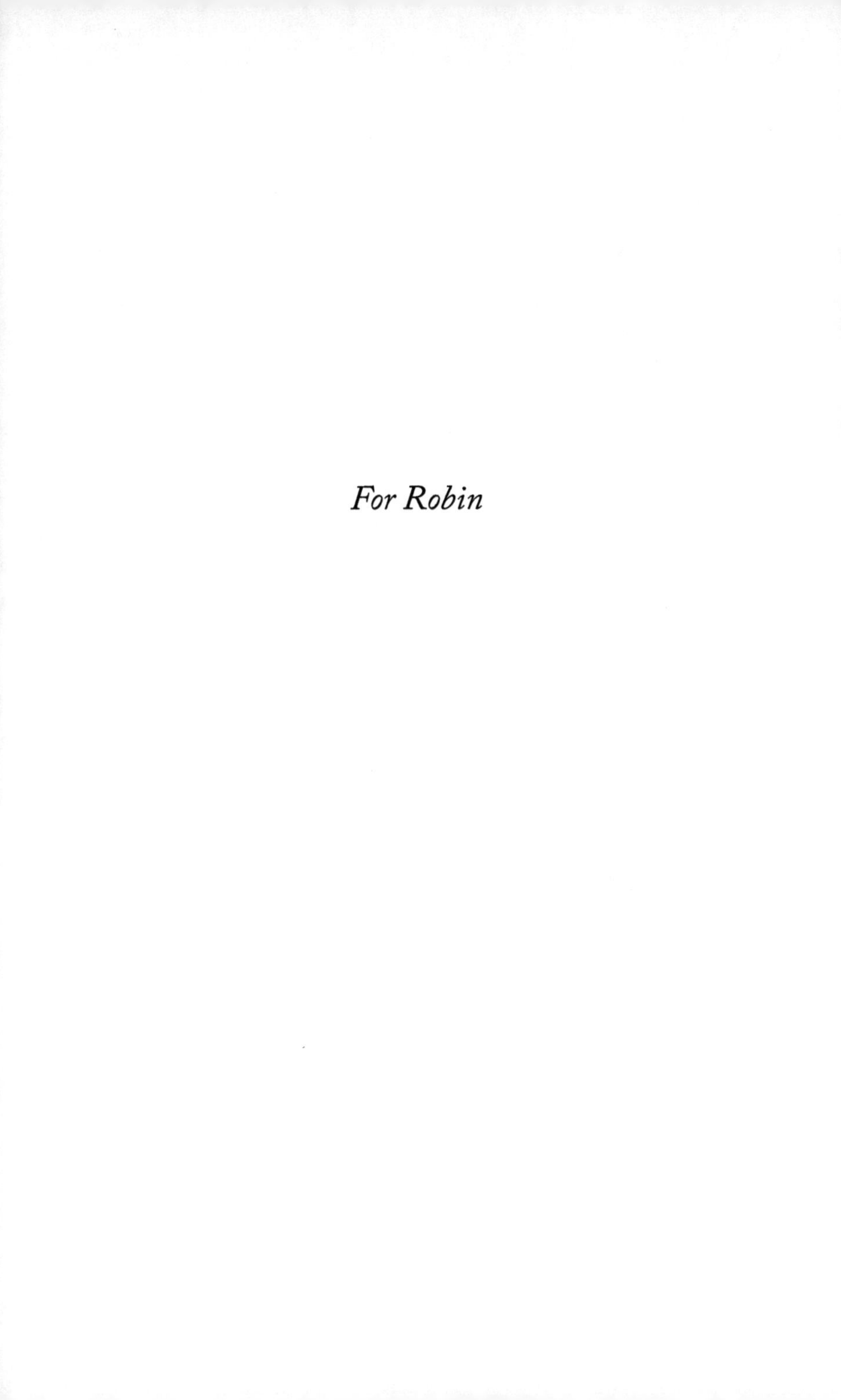

For Robin

One

On a warm late spring day with the trees on the Mall now in full blossom and many government workers in the nation's capital without overcoats, some men even without their jackets, the waiter of a small but pleasant restaurant just off Massachusetts Avenue brought coffee to one of a dozen sidewalk tables where two people were among a number seated there. One was young woman in a light tailored suit who was wearing heavy black-rimmed dark glasses and a large blue floppy sun hat that nearly hid her face. More anonymous in appearance than not, she could have been any one of many young women like her who worked in Washington for dozens of government agencies, foreign as well as American.

Seated almost primly erect, hands folded on the table directly before her, she was without any revealing physical expression as she listened to her companion, seated across from her. This was an older man who, dark-haired and slightly swarthy, had an air about him of executive importance. Immaculately tailored and groomed, he wore a modishly trimmed beard that was in keeping with his highly expensive Rolex chronometer wristwatch affixed on a gold band and his expensive gold cuff links. As he spoke in a lowered and cultivated voice, he would occasionally glance around, however, as though not wanting to be seen.

"The laundering chain," he explained, "is all part of an American-Russian plan to finance white supremacist groups in America, like the American Eagle and the Western Alliance, and in a coordinated program designed to provoke divisive instability via TV, Facebook, Instagram, and fake news rumor-mongering. The Russian bank in Riyadh, which invests in Saudi development—new skyscrapers, housing projects, etcetera—transferred a sum, reliably reported to be as much as two billion U.S. dollars, to a Saudi bank. The Saudi bank then transferred the money as an investment."

He paused to wiggle two fingers on each hand as quotation marks to indicate falsity, then continued.

"Not as stated in various Saudi Arabian development enterprises, but to a shell company in the Caribbean. From there it virtually disappeared into Mexico City, where it is invested in a Mexican company, Pro-Mex Metalurgia, which produces car parts. Pro-Mex then falsely listed the money as profit and invests it in varying small amounts over time, so as not to arouse Treasury

Department interest, in an outfit in Connecticut called Saugatuck Investments."

He paused, and the young woman spoke for the first time, her tone matter-of-fact.

"With all respect, sir, you're not telling us anything we don't already know. We've followed that money from Moscow all the way to Saugatuck Investments. You say American-Russian. Do you mean the plan originated in the United States, and if so, by whom?"

"In the U.S., yes. There's someone high up behind it all. We don't know whom. We only know of a vague code name: Nero."

"Nero? All right, we'll come back to that. The laundering again: you say that from Saugatuck Investments the laundered funds go directly to white nationalists and neo-Nazi militia groups?"

He shrugged. "As far as I know, that was its purpose."

"As far as you know? Sorry, let's have the rest. The State of Connecticut is not known to harbor illegitimate companies. Who, for a start, at Saugatuck is doing the dirty?"

"That, I can't say either. It's as far as my information goes."

The young woman smiled ingratiatingly in the shadow of her hat. It was her first show of emotion.

"Yes, you can. Now, come on. With all due respect, sir, if you're blowing whistles, blow them all the way. We guaranteed to totally respect your confidences."

He studied her. She was again patiently silent, looking straight back at him and waiting, and he saw a cold and determined hardness in her, in her downplayed makeup, in her slim athletic body, in her almost perfect facial features and expressionless eyes. He smiled thinly.

"You're a very persevering young lady."

She didn't answer.

"All right," he said. He took a breath. "At Saugatuck …"

He was drowned out by the blare of a taxicab horn close by as it was cut off by a motorcycle, which pulled up at the curb directly opposite the couple and only a few feet away. Bracing himself and the motionless bike with one heavily booted leg planted firmly on the curb, the bike's helmeted rider calmly pulled a .45 automatic from one of the saddle bags directly in back of his seat and above the bike's rear wheel, took careful aim, and pulled the trigger.

The shot hit the man that the young woman had just called a whistle-blower directly in the head, the heavy .45-caliber bullet blowing away nearly half of it. Blood, brains, and shards of bone and flesh flew everywhere over the white tablecloth before him, some spattering on her while his deceased body remained mawkishly erect, one manicured hand on the table still cupped around his half-finished coffee.

A roar of sound. The bike was gone. There was a moment of intense and terrible silence. Only the noise of still passing traffic was heard.

Then a woman screamed and bedlam followed. Panicked customers and staff, thinking it a terrorist attack, milled about both inside the restaurant and out, some pushing their way among the tables, knocking them over and crowding to the back of the place, trying to find a place to hide; others, in flight, took blindly to the street.

Seemingly unfazed, the young woman rose with surprising calmness, quickly took her shoulder bag from the chair next to her, slung it loosely over her shoulder, and forcing her way through knots of screaming customers and overturned tables, got herself into the women's restroom, where she immediately locked herself in and, ignoring desperate pounding on the door, wetted a handful of paper towels, and in seconds had wiped clean her face and the front of her dress.

Finished, she checked the presence of a small handgun in her shoulder bag, then left the restroom and exited the restaurant, pushing her way through the still terrified customers, too traumatized to flee. Out on the sidewalk she headed down the street away from the restaurant at a determinedly fast walk without even glancing at the still seated corpse with which, only moments before, she'd been conversing, and which, when living, had been Prince Mohammed Adi, a member of the Saudi royal family.

Not more than a minute had passed since the fatal shot was fired. Less than two minutes more, and as the first wails of sirens from police cars and ambulances began to be heard, the young woman had put a good distance between herself and the chaos she had just left. Without looking back, she pulled up short at a bar that was virtually empty, its few patrons out on the street craning to see what had happened. She grabbed a stool, ordered herself a large straight shot of vodka, downed it instantly, and then, hands covering her face, suddenly succumbed to an almost violent trembling of her whole body while gasping for breath.

Her name was Kelsie Gordon. She was thirty-four years old and an undercover agent with an investigative branch of FinCen, the Financial Crime Enforcement Network department of the United States Treasury.

She was also a daughter of the vice president of the United States.

Two

"Mohammed Adi never gave you any names at Saugatuck?"

"No."

"You're absolutely certain of that."

"Yes."

"Not even a hint?"

"Nothing."

"Any other names besides those you have well documented while chasing the money from Moscow to the USA?"

"None."

"Or who this Nero was who Adi said was behind the whole dirty project in the first place?"

"Just the obvious code name."

"You did well to get that, at least."

The meeting took place in a secure room at the headquarters of FinCen in Vienna, Virginia, a suburb of Washington, DC, and it was late evening, the same day. One speaker was Marie Suarez, a stocky, authoritative woman dressed in a slightly severe tailored suit. A gray-haired steely veteran head of the covert investigative unit at

FinCen, she had come to Treasury from the CIA, where she'd worked in counterintelligence. Before that she had been a detective investigating homicides for the Chicago police force.

With a no-nonsense reputation, Suarez had seen everything in the covert world as well as in the overt, and had about her an air of perpetual irony that bordered on disbelief of anything that was not hard proven fact. Added to that was a self-imposed wall of silence about herself that shut out any knowledge of her private life, if indeed she even had one, and was constantly speculated on by her staff. It was as though she had simply been planted behind her desk and had no life at all beyond the four walls of her office, which were bare save for a television monitor.

The other was Kelsie Gordon, her relationship to the vice president unknown even after a routine FBI background check. She had first studied at the John Jay College of Criminal Justice in New York. She then had spent some relatively long years at the DA's office in Brooklyn on the trail of Mafia crimes where, as an undercover investigator, she had established a reputation for toughness.

Present also was Charles Wheeler, a deputy of the unit's communications and information section. In sharp contrast to Suarez, he was a slender man in his fifties who wore a colorful bow tie and had elitist origins at Princeton and the Woodrow Wilson International School, where he had studied both Russian and Arabic.

He had come to Treasury ten years previous from the Brookings Institute, where he had been a fellow in Mideast studies, and only recently—three years ago—had come to FinCen. Widely traveled and speaking four languages, he was advisor to agents, covert as well as overt.

A fourth at the meeting, Joshua Marshall, struck a different chord. Seemingly quiet and reserved in nature, he was a near giant Black man in his sixties, his hair graying. A graduate of Howard University, he had rowed two-man shells and had reached international competition at Henley in England, where he'd taken a second against the German team. He was an expert on white nationalism and white supremacist groups and was on the proscribed list of several for execution after he had been discovered secretly videotaping a meeting of one of the more virulent neo-Nazi militias in Pennsylvania. He had come to FinCen from the SPLC, the Southern Poverty Law Center, the nation's unquestioned authority on racism and white supremacy.

Sitting across from Kelsie, Marshall mentally ticked off her tracking large sums of laundered Russian money. More than a billion had eventually arrived in the USA, and she'd spent the past six months as a "cultural attaché" at the U.S. embassy in Moscow, as well as with Fin-Cen operatives at the U.S. embassy in Brussels and at EU headquarters. Finally, she'd worked in Riyadh, in Saudi Arabia. She'd been back in Washington less than two weeks.

Before yesterday's "incident," as she termed it, she'd discovered and reported Mohammed Adi to be involved in suspicious transactions between Deutsche Bank and a nonexistent Caribbean shell company. Finding him in the United States along with the laundered money, she'd contacted him, and he'd expected his possible whistle-blowing to get himself off the Deutsche Bank hook, but not his murder. She seemed surprisingly unaffected by it.

Wheeler said, "This code name, Nero, that Adi mentioned. You're positive he didn't even hint as to whom or to what it might apply?"

"Positive."

Suarez said to Wheeler, "Charles, look for it in our database on codes." And to Marshall, "And can you check SPLC files in case there's a white supremacist Nero buried someplace?" Then back to Kelsie, "Do you think the shooter got a look at you, Miss Gordon? That concerns me."

"No."

Wheeler laughed. "She was hiding under a big blue floppy hat. The TV crowd are having a field day with it."

Suarez had no patience for frivolity and wasn't amused. She said rather coldly, "The police too," before asking Kelsie about the shooter's ID.

"No identifiable person? Nobody you'd ever run across before at any time?"

"Correct."

"Age?"

"Fiftyish."

"Hair color?"

"He was wearing a black helmet."

"Skin?"

"Caucasian. Pale, partially bearded."

"Any shot at nationality?"

"Possibly Russian."

"Tall? Short?"

"Medium."

"What kind of bike?"

"Honda. Powerful. 500 cc."

"He shouted nothing?"

"He was laughing."

Wheeler said, "Sick bastard." And added, to Kelsie, "Good thing he didn't get you too. Maybe your hat put him off."

"And maybe not," Suarez said. She rose abruptly and slapped a file closed. "Meeting adjourned. I'll see all three of you here again tomorrow at oh eight thirty."

Getting to his car in the building parking lot, Marshall thought, *Suarez has met her match when it comes to ice. That girl has enough chill for a dozen. "Yes, no, yes, no." Surreal. Freezer cold like she'd never been spattered with brains.*

Stuck in traffic on the way home, and waiting impatiently for one light after another to turn from red to green, he thought back on his mildly protesting Suarez from keeping her on the job any further. Tough as hell, yes. But people had their limits.

"Marie, she's pretty wiped out."

"Think so?"

"If not, she should be."

"It's too late for a replacement."

"Sure?"

"We're budget-cut shorthanded, Josh, and someone new would have too many ropes to pick up on. Besides, she's onto this Nero, whoever he is. We need to find that out."

He'd reluctantly surrendered. "Next step, then?"

"Connecticut. The Saugatuck Investment Company."

Once Marshall was well on the beltway, traffic lessened, and NPR was going on about the latest on the president's ill health as he branched off it for his modest frame home in middle-class Takoma Park. *Old guy is going to kick off before his term is finished,* he thought, *and we'll be stuck with the religious nut VP.*

He was met at the door by his wife, Elaine, who held out an ice-cold tall glass of tequila, his favorite end-of-the-day drink.

"Traffic bad?"

"Murder."

"Speaking of which?"

"Don't."

"Then I guessed right. The guy blown away. The gal in the big blue floppy hat. She's one of yours?"

"You're psychic."

"No. The clue was the Arab. You told me you were following money through Riyadh. And once you said she was there."

Joshua laughed. His wife was a perfect fit for the intelligence work at FinCen, except she worked for a senator. He came into the living room, dumped his dispatch case, and sank into his favorite chair, automatically remoting as he did to CNN. Erin Burnett was holding forth about the day's events, but he found his mind elsewhere. Connecticut was hardly Central America, and the Saugatuck Investment Company, where the money had apparently come to rest, had a good reputation. It was one of half a dozen such firms mostly specializing in hedge funds and taking advantage of Connecticut's tax laws. Hosting blue-chip clients, they lined the banks of the Saugatuck River, which ran through the middle of Westport, an affluent, midsize, semi-suburban town on Long Island Sound that was partially a dormitory for New York City, an hour's commute away.

Saugatuck's board, besides several Wall Street heavy hitters who had been checked out as blameless, counted three members that he remembered as fringing on white nationalism, although nothing definite had been proven. The same was true of Saugatuck's president, Anthony Bellistree, who had made a fortune in hedge funds for himself and a small host of famous clients. Joshua had nagging doubts about Bellistree. The SPLC had received a vague report of his possible association with white supremacists, and it was worrying that Vice President Emanuel Arthur was a major Saugatuck client and had been for years.

The CEO of Saugatuck Investments, whose god was money, seemed an odd pick for investment advice by the devout evangelist Vice President Emanuel Arthur. Now going gray, he was a handsome man save for a perpetual expression of correctness, as though he would never for any reason step out of the righteous religiosity with which he surrounded himself. Certainly, he had never shown any affinity for any extremist right-wing ideology. But had he been targeted by extremists as susceptible to their vitriol, and thus of possible innocent help to their agendas?

The report had never gone anywhere, but Joshua had always wondered. Aware that his wife had settled nearby, he weighed her working for a senator, and his need, and said, "Favor?"

"What?"

"You have friends in the FBI. I want to know if you could not ask someone there if they have anything filed away someplace on one billionaire, or near billionaire, Anthony Bellistree, other than his banking success."

"Why not ask them yourself?"

"And get my head chopped if Marie Suarez found out I had. We and they are competitors, remember?"

"Well, remember I'm not supposed to ever divulge."

"Understood. But smell around anyway."

A laugh, meaning she would, and he was left with his thoughts about Agent Gordon again.

He wondered how she'd go about ferreting out just exactly which business or manufacturing concerns, as Saugatuck clients, might be a cover for financing white nationalist false news, false facts, false rumors, and a dozen other divisive tricks beneficial to the Russians and the Chinese. Whatever someone at Saugatuck was doing, it had to be well buried, and she had her work cut out for her.

Three

The narrow little two-story frame house was crammed between two just like it in a row of them on a quiet tree-lined street off Lincoln Park, behind the Capitol and Union Station. Once an area quartering freed slaves working at the Navy Yard and in building the Capitol, some of it had gentrified its way slowly upward to become a peaceful neighborly refuge for government workers choosing to avoid the commute from suburbs like Takoma Park or Potomac to any of a dozen massive government buildings crammed between Massachusetts and Constitution Avenues.

Kelsie Gordon parked her old and weathered car, out of habit glanced quickly at the street around her—it was empty, save for a mother pushing twins in a double stroller, and a postal van—then went up the three stone steps to the door. She'd long ago become accustomed to the house she and her brother, Gareth, had inherited from their mother being just as unimportant as her neighbors'. Except for the few years she'd spent in New York at college and working, she and Gareth had lived in it for as long as she could remember, and she felt more than lucky to have its roof over their heads. Upkeep expenses were still low enough to be handled by the salary of a mid-level civil servant, and in the peaceful quiet close to nearby Stanton Park, where many of her neighbors were civil workers like herself, she could live as anonymously as she did in her professional life.

Getting out her keys, Kelsie felt the cold hardness of her little .22-caliber Beretta Minx and wished she'd had the presence of mind to pull it and shoot the bike rider before he'd got away—preferably to kneecap him or otherwise render him seriously incapacitated. Alive, he could have proved useful in further investigation.

"Fucking bastard," she muttered. Snuggling the Beretta even deeper into the side pocket of her handbag, where it was always kept, she tried not to think yet again of the jarring shot, the dark, rather handsome head disintegrating right in front of her, the blood, the brains, the awful silence, and then all the screaming, and above all, the jeering laughter of the shooter as he calmly put the heavy automatic back into the leather saddlebag above the rear wheel of the motorbike.

"Where the hell were you, then?" she said aloud to the little Beretta before she unlocked the door and went inside.

On entering, she briefly felt the lingering cloak of her work, and then, as always, began to mentally push it away, and to do what she always did when work was over and she came home. She began to change one identity for another. She became family, her and Gareth, just the two of them, Gareth twelve years younger.

Once, they'd been more complete. Once, there had been four. There'd been her and Gareth, their mother, Andrea, dying of a virulent cancer, and Angel Savannah, her final days nurse. Then Andrea was no longer there, gone forever, and there were just her and Gareth and Angel, who for years took her place as their guardian, until finally Angel too was gone. Kelsie had put fresh flowers on her and Andrea's graves the moment she'd returned from abroad.

With Gareth now just finishing up at the American University and planning medical school, he too might soon be gone. Then there would only be one—herself. The thought was nearly unbearable. Nothing would be left in life except the sick world she worked in, and being as anonymous in what she did as she was otherwise.

She went directly into the little living room-library that shared most of the ground floor with the kitchen and a stair to two bedrooms above. The room was cluttered, the furniture getting old, the curtains and carpeting in need of replacement. There were books everywhere, and some of Gareth's lacrosse equipment scattered about. He was on the varsity team. In a packed bookcase that fully occupied one wall, there was a framed photograph of Angel. Sandwiched between books, it stared at Kelsie with a soft and loving look, and was inscribed "Love, Angel."

Kelsie lifted the photo from among the books and studied it a moment before gently kissing it and saying, "I'm home, Angel." When she spoke, she was no longer the cold undercover agent seen by her colleagues. She was the girl who, after the brutal murder of the whistleblower, had sat alone in a bar and had broken down. The icy coldness fell away before the quiet resignation of the end of a hard day. It fled a lonely and anxious woman whom life had forced to be a "mom" and the family breadwinner when in reality she was only a big sister.

Putting the photo back, she went to a minifridge, took out a bottle of ice-cold vodka, poured a double shot in a glass, and headed for the couch, her heart flooding with memories of Angel's richly smooth dark-brown skin, of her softly gentle eyes and caressing hands, of her quiet musical voice filled with love.

And getting settled, she remembered how, after Andrea had gone, Angel had worked part-time at the hospital on a morning shift to earn money for their food and clothing and to pay utilities. Then how, when she and Gareth came home from school, there were always fresh baked cookies to hold them while she helped them with their homework until she fixed dinner. And finally, how she'd always read to them or watched their favorite TV shows with them until it was bedtime, and when, after tucking them in, she went back to the hospital for another shift late at night while a friend came and babysat.

Throughout, Angel had never complained, not even once, of the bitterly hard life she'd lived in her own childhood in the Deep South, where her sharecropper father and her mother had toiled day and night in the cotton fields to make money to send her to a church school, her never-ending determination to reward them and their tears of pride when she was capped as a registered nurse.

With weariness of the day flowing over her like a dark tide, Kelsie looked for the news channel, but instead of the news got a speech by her father, his legitimate daughter Corinna by his side and radiant from one of the many business deals she'd won thanks to her father's influence. Kelsie quickly switched the TV off again, muttering wearily, "Bastard," and trying not to think of either of them.

But she found it hard not to. It was ever more difficult to hear the endless lies, false facts, and distortions of reality that her father preached to his political base, or his sycophancy toward the ailing occupant of the White House who was twice the man he was or ever could be. She couldn't turn on the TV at any time, day or night, without hearing him, but she had painfully learned to suppress the helpless rage she felt toward him when she did and whenever it bitingly rose within her.

She'd been eighteen and just starting college on a full scholarship when, in despair at forever being told, first by her mother, then by Angel, that her father had died before she was born, but never who he was or anything else about him, she'd decided on a search, and was appealing to television's ancestry program when Angel finally relented. Her mother, when a college student, Angel said, had interned for Emanuel Arthur, then a first-term congressman and already long married. When pregnancy had resulted from their brief affair, Emanuel, terrified that news of it would ruin him, had bought off Andrea's silence with a home put in her name, a threat to take her child away if she ever breathed a word, and legal maneuvers to extinguish any trace of his parentage as well as Andrea's.

A subsequent brief encounter by a lonely Andrea with an unknown lover, when she was showing first signs of the cancer that had killed her, had produced Gareth twelve years later.

Evading Capitol police, Kelsie remembered, she had confronted her father in his congressional office. When, in response to his demanding to know who she was, and she'd come right out and said, "I'm your daughter," his reaction was intense. He had denied any knowledge of her mother or her, and his angry shouted words still burned. "If you ever bother me again with your vicious scam, you nasty little crook, I'll have you arrested."

She had been forcibly removed by the police

and had taking legal advice. Like her father's disavowal, the lawyer's words still burned. "You have no legal proof he's your father, only Angel's word, which is legally unacceptable hearsay," and she was advised to forget it. Emanuel Arthur was fast becoming politically powerful and talked of one day becoming president. "He can destroy any independent future for both you and your brother if provoked."

Convinced her father's disavowal was a crime, and with hope one day of proving it, she'd scrapped an application for college in Washington and applied to the John Jay School of Criminal Justice in New York, where she'd elected criminology as a major with criminal justice as a minor. She'd excelled and had taken a first job offer from the district attorney's office in Brooklyn.

Kelsie finished the vodka, and muttering aloud, "For Christ sake, Kelsie, stop rutting around in the past. It's done, finished, over with," she rose and poured another. The two days she'd just lived had left her thoughts drained of clarity, and it was with a start that she realized that in the past twenty-four hours she hadn't given one thought to Gareth. Where on earth was he? His last class at the American University would have finished hours ago.

Four

She found a note he'd left on the kitchen table saying he'd be late. Some of his friends were throwing a party in Bethesda. He might even hit a couch at their pad, he said, and catch an Uber home in the morning. Her heart nearly stopped. She'd come back from Europe to find him recovering from an OD two weeks before and being monitored by a rehab therapist. He was now off drugs, everyone thought, but when barely back home, and the day before she met with the Saudi, she'd discovered a small bag of heroin in his sock drawer. She'd had it out with him, pouring the heroin down the toilet as he stood numbly watching.

"Gareth, you promised."

"Sorry."

"Sorry's not good enough. You promised me and the rehab therapist. How are we supposed to help you if you ignore us?"

"Sorry."

The second "sorry" infuriated her. She'd lost her temper. It was the kind of defense Gareth had always thrown up ever since a little boy when he didn't want to face reality.

She'd screamed at him, "Sorry, my butt. What kind of a goddamned fool are you? Gareth, you're not a little boy any longer. You're a senior in college, soon to graduate, and planning medical school. This stuff's poison, and you're killing yourself with it. Don't you want to live? What the fucking hell are you doing at university if you want to die?" And then, "If you can't kick this shit for yourself, what about me? Do you really want to set me up for your funeral? Thanks a lot."

It had ended up as always with her and Gareth in tears and in each other's arms. She'd sent him off to the rehab therapist and had got assurance that Gareth was back on the wagon and she could spend a while without worrying. But she wondered if it would never stop. Addiction was a way of life to addicts, she'd been told. If you stopped an addict from feeding himself the poison, you took his life away, and they'd fight, as anyone would fight for their life, to hang onto theirs with another pill or another shot. But there was hope, his therapist had also told her. Gareth was on his way back from permanent addiction, he was sure. His will to live was strong in him, and with patience, drugs would eventually be a thing of the past.

She made herself dinner and ate in silence without turning on the TV again, instead worrying about Gareth and bills she'd neglected that had to be paid. What she'd thought to be an easy and quiet job when she'd first come to Fin-Cen—she'd never met a civil servant who killed themselves working—and a final escape from the nightmare she'd daily lived when working undercover for the Brooklyn DA, where the horror and killing in the Mafia world had become for her a long dragged-out nightmare. She was one of the few who could do what she did, but she had soon wearied of what had started out in Brooklyn as an adventure before turning into a reality, and which saw her typed with little chance that any of her superiors would ever see her any other way.

Meanwhile, with Gareth's huge student loan and his plans for medical school looming, she was his sole support. And perhaps she would still be even afterward, before he could earn enough as a doctor to pay for his becoming one. Even though nonpolitical government jobs like hers were relatively secure, you had to watch your back. Neither she nor he had inherited anything from their impoverished mother except the house, and from Angel the few hundred dollars she'd somehow managed to save and which had all gone for her funeral. She'd shut any conceivably possible door for her ever receiving a penny from their father when, before being thrown from his office, she'd delivered a stinging slap to his face, and in front of his entire staff had told him to go fuck himself.

She'd never told Gareth any of it—not who their father was, nor how he'd come to be, nor how she'd learned. She'd only told him that Angel's death made her alone responsible for him.

The phone rang. It was Marie Suarez. Work swept back over Kelsie in an unwanted flood. Jesus, what the hell did *she* want?

"Sorry to reach you at home. Are you okay?"

Tell her you're okay. Tell her to take the damn job and stuff it. "Sure. I'm fine."

"Reminder call. You left before I could tell you. We've got officialdom tomorrow. Eight o'clock sharp. Okay?"

"Sure."

"Good."

The phone clicked. Kelsie stared at the dead receiver, then got up and went and poured herself another vodka. She'd started drinking too much, she knew, and ought to cut back. This had to be the last one tonight, because if she went on there'd be more than one; there'd be two, even three, and she couldn't afford a hangover because she knew from experience exactly what officialdom tomorrow would bring. She'd been involved, one way or another, in other incidents of a sensational nature, while working for the DA in Brooklyn, that had threatened her anonymity. At no time ever had anybody discovered she was the vice president's daughter, and this case would be no different.

Tomorrow there'd be Suarez and almost certainly Suarez's own boss, "Mace" Armstrong, and other superiors. There'd be Wheeler and Marshall, the higher-up police too, of course, like the WPD boss. There'd also be, also almost certainly, some big shot or other from Treasury seeing a threat to himself, and perhaps, more than a threat, a howl from the White House. There'd also quite likely be an official from the Saudi embassy, although, if so, the Saudi position on anything would be, "Sorry, you're asking for top-secret information we can't possibly give you."

The whole meeting would be a wasteful farce. Afterward, the police would then issue a report to the press saying the same thing: that the shooting involved a nameless informant whose identity, along with that of the woman with him, could not be revealed without threatening national security. The media would scream foul and suppression of free speech for a week and then get bored with it all and turn to something easier. Soon the horrifying incident of a man whose head had been blasted half off while having coffee at a respectable sidewalk café on a quiet sunny morning with some unknown young woman would be forgotten.

Five

Oh eight thirty in the morning: It was just as Kelsie had envisioned. The superintendent of police came, a big shot from Treasury came representing the Secretary of the Treasury himself, and a couple of bored guys from fairly high up the FBI ladder tagged along. Saudi people, trying to look Western, did too. It lasted nearly two hours, and when the why of the shooting and the identity of the girl in the big blue floppy hat were swept under the proverbial carpet, everyone heaved a sigh of relief.

In such meetings, especially when there was potential scandal, everyone in FinCen had long since learned, even high-ranking Suarez to be tactfully low-key before an avalanche of their superiors. When they had finally all gone, however, and with Kelsie's anonymity intact, along with FinCen's assured reputation not even scratched, Suarez dropped the mask of career civil servant correctness she'd worn in the face of those of higher rank than her but who had little knowledge of the complex work in the department she governed. Wheeler loosened his ridiculous bow tie, and Joshua Marshall, who had been mostly silent throughout, got out his laptop.

Suarez said, "Joshua?"

Marshall turned to a silent Kelsie. "Miss Gordon, you've been working on this case in relatively refined Europe, embassies, banks and so on, where people are civilized, at least outwardly. There was little serious danger to you. You worked before that in the far different nastiness of those areas in New York that are Mafia family crime-ridden. I'll not dismiss any danger there to you; I'm sure there was plenty. The brutality of the various Mafia, especially toward anyone who tries to control them, is notorious, but even so I don't think, in my experience, it compares to what you might well face from various neo-Nazi white supremacists and super nationalist militia groups you could possibly encounter in this case, if they should get onto your investigating them.

"To give you some idea, and as a caution to you, I want to show you the following. Some of it is stock footage, some recorded by me while I was with the SPLC, and for which I'm on a hit list."

Joshua scrolled his laptop and light suddenly appeared on the TV monitor on the wall directly across from Marie Suarez's desk. Pictures appeared of marching, chanting men wearing swastika arm bands, carrying Nazi banners and fiery torches and chanting, "Burn all Jews."

Joshua said, "We've all seen group pictures like this. Now for closer shots." The scene changed to a single man on a podium giving the Nazi salute. Behind him, swastika banners. "Okay for this view of their leader too, but how about this same guy when above the surface?" The picture changed to a respectable businessman addressing a harmless club function. "Or these fellows here," Joshua said, "in their fellow-citizen lives."

Quick shots followed of several quite ordinary people, a farmer, a shopkeeper, a schoolteacher, a garage owner. "And here," Joshua said, "the same four at playtime." Pictures of the men appeared, but now they were heavily armed and wearing camouflage battle dress as they furtively practiced an attack on an unseen enemy in a heavily wooded area. "Militias," Joshua explained. "There are perhaps fifty groups spread out all over the country, preparing for the day when they will storm Washington and take over the government."

He paused briefly while the men practiced war, and then said, "What you will see next was shot clearly from hiding and with a long-range lens and super sensitive film. It was seized while I was still at the SPLC in a raid on the office of a presumably respectable warehouse manager. We found several more of the same that were cleverly hidden at home by a local car salesman. Respectable men enjoying themselves, in different places and at different times, torturing and gang-raping young women."

What followed on the TV monitor was so

horrendous that Suarez finally rose to tell Joshua to shut it down. She was too late; the film had come to an end, leaving Kelsie, Wheeler, and Suarez herself trying to forget what they had seen.

It was night, and the film first showed a pickup truck as it drew up to an abandoned factory building. Two tied-up young women were dragged from the back of the pickup by half a dozen men who were drinking heavily. They were taken inside, where they were next seen in a space filled with dormant heavy machinery. As they vainly struggled, they were stripped naked and shackled to a long-dead heavy lathe. With the men grinning and laughing and crowding in close around them, some forcibly forced the long necked whiskey bottles into their vaginas. A blowtorch was lit and one of the men began to use it on their screaming victims, at first on their legs from a distance, then closer and rising up to the whiskey bottles so that smoke from burning flesh filled the air.

In the dead silence that filled the reality of Suarez's office, Joshua closed his laptop and said, "I think you saw enough to tell you that behind a mask of respectability in this country, we have our share of utter savagery."

He turned to Kelsie. "The people you have just seen are not necessarily those awaiting the money you have traced all the way from Moscow to here, but their character and thinking are the same, and you shouldn't forget it for one moment, no matter how respectable Saugatuck Investments might seem. But someone there is someone of their kind, and more than likely directed by someone elsewhere, higher up—Russian, American, who knows?—quite possibly the latter. Probably your Nero person has his finger on more than willing big finance and its hidden transfer, and whose bright idea it is to use it to create divisiveness and hate throughout the country in Russia's favor."

He pushed aside the coffee he'd been drinking. "Miss Gordon, I probably don't need to say it, but you should be extremely careful not ever to let yourself be pulled into one of these white nationalist group's meetings."

Six

Joshua took a file from his briefcase, opened it, and extracted a half-dozen glossy photographs, which he fanned out across the smooth surface of Marie Suarez's desk. He said, again directly to Kelsie, "One shot fired and then flight in little more than a second or two doesn't give much time for ID, Miss Gordon, I understand that. But just in case, browse these. They're pictures of white supremacists we know to be hit men."

Kelsie stared down at the half-dozen four-by-five glossy photos of different men, all of them white and at ages that varied from around thirty-five to sixty. She had barely glanced at them when she stabbed a finger at one.

"That one."

"Sure?"

"Positive."

The photograph showed an almost albino blondness in the thinning hair, tied back in a pigtail, and the long sideburns of a middle-aged man whose mouth was a thin, nearly lipless line above a weak chin on which there was a narrow goatee. There were several old Soviet Union–style hammer-and-sickles tattooed on bare muscular arms that belied a growing paunch, along with a swastika on his chest.

Seeing the picture, Kelsie for a moment was swept away from the room around her. Everything dimmed. Her interlocutors suddenly seemed far off, their voices meaningless and echoing. There was only the face and the shot.

"Kelsie?"

And she heard Marshall saying, "That's a guy named Grigori Lebedev. We've had him on our books for quite a while. He's suspected of a number of killings, especially throughout the West, Washington State, Nevada, and Arizona. He's a Russian, of all things, and he's wanted in his own country as well as here, although we believe he's protected there by someone high up whom the police don't dare to challenge. Possibly in this country also, since he seems free to come and go as he pleases. The Southern Poverty Law Center spotted him six months ago with an especially violent and outright Nazi group, the Colonial Eagles, who are based somewhere in Massachusetts."

"Not enough hard evidence for an arrest?" Wheeler offered.

"Probably not. Nor a trial."

Suarez said, "Russian, is he? And apparently protected?" She was thoughtful a moment while Marshall and Wheeler waited, and then said,

"Do you suppose that somehow he could possibly be tied in to Putin's pal, Boris Sokolov?"

Wheeler looked surprised and laughed. "Sokolov, the billionaire oil baron? Marie, you're not serious. Just because they're both Russian?"

"I'm dead serious," she said. "The FBI has Lebedev in several places in Russia at the same time as Sokolov. And over here too, during several of Sokolov's visits. But all right, that doesn't concern me right now. Hit men, American Nazis, Russians, or otherwise are Joshua's affair. My concern is elsewhere. We haven't so far overly paid attention to who in Russia might be the source of what Miss Gordon has discovered laundered half way around the world, and I find I'm thinking of Sokolov possibly being the one.

"The amount of time he spends in this country is no secret. Everyone knows how enamored he has become of everything American. Look how often he vacations with the VP at Emanuel Arthur's trout fishing hideaway in Maine, and, according to the FBI, once at the same time as a visit there by Saugatuck Investments' Bellistree. What better way to turn billions into more billions than investing in legitimate hedge funds in Connecticut, yes, but is that what Bellistree, a white supremacist suspect, was there for? Investing? There's too much in all of this not to make one suspicious."

"She's right," Joshua Marshall said to Wheeler, who looked dubious. "And as long as we're talking about Sokolov, equally interesting to me is what on earth he has in common with the vice president, unless he's using him somehow, with the VP naively unaware. Emanuel Arthur wears Jesus-freak evangelism on his sleeve like a giant identity badge. Struts around that huge church in Iowa like he had sole ownership of God. And, I suspect, totally unaware of the evil around him."

"Or plain not wanting to know if it's there," Suarez said.

The sudden talk of the vice president caught Kelsie off guard. She instantly felt her long and carefully guarded anonymity threatened. And at the same time realized how desperately tired she was of making an endless effort to swallow the self-destroying hate that came over her in waves even at the very mention of her father's name.

She stood abruptly and said as calmly as she could, "I think I am unnecessarily wasting your time. At this point I can't recall a single additional thing of interest I could offer. Perhaps when I'll have Charles's briefing, if any, on the Connecticut company I'm going to?"

Slightly taken back by such abrupt and icy firmness, which she wasn't used to in an employee, Suarez, with equal abrupt firmness, said, "We'd like to send you off immediately, if you can manage it, Miss Gordon. Charles thinks it's important not to delay with things possibly in a turmoil due to the assassination. Could you manage tomorrow?"

"Tomorrow? Of course." Kelsie's heart sank. Gareth. She'd wanted to spend several days with him.

"Charles?" Suarez said, turning to Wheeler.

"I'll get to her later, perhaps tomorrow, before she leaves," Wheeler said, and to Kelsie, "I've some groundwork to do first, with your immediate contact there, where you'll be staying."

There was a pause, and then Kelsie heard, "Are you sure, now? I mean about going. I could try to find somebody else." There was an unexpected tone in Marie Suarez's voice: concern. For human reasons? Or, after such a shakeup, for job capability?

Kelsie saw it as the latter. Suarez was too tough for concern. *Doesn't go with the job,* she thought, *and something I never got in Moscow either, for all the embassy so-called politeness, and especially not in that shitty god-awful Riyadh, with all their hateful "keep women in slavery for breeding only." Nor in Brussels, wading through mostly male bureaucratic horseshit for what seemed forever, and like some of them had never heard of women.*

She said to Wheeler, "Are you texting me, or are we meeting?"

"Probably the latter."

"Thank you. Keep me posted." Kelsie grabbed up her handbag from where she'd hung it over the back of her chair, as she perpetually did everywhere, nodded at the others, and without another word, silently left the room.

When she'd gone, Charles Wheeler let out a

low whistle. "Wow … I wouldn't want to get in her sights."

Joshua Marshall said, "Agreed, but she's more than likely just exhausted. She's handled enough along the way on this case better than if we'd put three on the job."

"Yeah, but like every other agent undercover, she lives in her own world. Self-imposed isolation. Don't be identified, don't admit, don't tell. I'm anonymous."

"Part of the job," Marie Suarez agreed. She thought that she probably ought to override Kelsie. The white supremacists she might well come up against weren't European bureaucrats, and she didn't want the scandal of having one of her female employees taken captive by them, if that should happen. The government was still largely male-oriented, and many saw women as frail, with a need to be protected, not sent into danger. But she didn't like the idea of fighting with Kelsie over it. She was too valuable to them to create unnecessary issues and, for a start, somebody else wouldn't know half what she knew on the case. That could make everything they'd learned so far information that would have to be relearned.

She said crisply, "I'll leave briefing her to you, Charles. Your contact in Connecticut, even if useful, is more than unusual. Are you quite sure of it?"

Wheeler said, "Very. She's in our pocket all the way."

"But she's an idiot social butterfly. Or at least the press bills her that way, and she certainly looks and acts like one."

"Don't be fooled, Marie. What you're seeing behind Melissa Paulstein's inscrutable mask isn't so much stupidity as vanity personified, which is exactly why she can be used so easily. And besides that, what we're getting from her, other than this connection for Gordon, is invaluable."

"Let's hope you're right." Marie rose. "Keep me posted. Meeting adjourned."

Seven

In the evening of the same day, and as the sun was setting over Connecticut, Jermyn Ortega, still at work, was rudely interrupted in thoughts of his distant native Guatemala by the sharp biting sting on his face from gravel thrown up by the wheels of the heavy car that passed only a foot away from the bed of pansies he was on his knees weeding at the side of the long tailored driveway. As an illegal immigrant, one of the army of thousands who tended the properties of wealthy New Englanders from New York to Maine, he was too imbued with fear of deportation to become angry and curse. Numbly resigned, he simply sat back, and with a soiled handkerchief pulled from his jeans, dabbed at blood that oozed from several small cuts on his forehead and scalp before resuming his weeding.

The offending vehicle was a top-of-the-line chauffeur-driven Rolls Royce convertible owned by the disgraced billionaire financier Herbert Paulstein. The sole passenger, whom the uniformed chauffeur rushed around to help from the leather interior of the spacious back seats, was Paulstein's wife, Melissa. Slender and only just out of her twenties, her straight dark hair cut stylishly neck-length, she could have been, in appearance and with the inscrutable lack of expression on her classically beautiful face, any of a score of top fashion models just returned from being photographed for *Vogue* magazine and wearing the latest creation of some famous designer.

With neither a word nor a nod to the chauffeur, she quickly went up the wide stone steps to the massive oak front door of the palatial mansion that was Soundview and home, and which, over the years, had welcomed many of the most prominent among the nation's celebrities and politicians, along with world-class financiers and politicians. Besides harboring twenty bedrooms and several large reception rooms as well as a library, a screening room, and an indoor swimming pool, it was also home to a discreetly tucked-away three-room business office used by the disgraced owner as well as an equivalent one for both his and his wife's personal affairs.

Melissa had no need to reach for the handle of the heavy door. The door magically opened before she had got to it, revealing when it did a primly reverent maid in a starched uniform and white cap. She didn't speak until Melissa was inside the spacious front hall, and then only to ask if she'd be dining alone that evening.

Stripping off white kid gloves to reveal a mani-cured hand graced by diamond engagement and wedding rings, and a wrist half-hidden by a wide diamond-and-emerald bracelet that matched an equivalent glittering necklace and earrings, Melissa answered with a curt "Yes," and then added, "I'll have a drink on the terrace first. My usual. Tell William."

"Yes, madam."

The maid departed on the errand, Melissa glanced briefly at herself in the ornate mirror over the long marble hall table, then crossed the wide hall itself to enter the equally spacious liv-ing room that had been expensively furnished and decorated by a famous Hollywood designer. After passing through one of several French doors, she dropped onto a gaily decorated lounge chair on a wide flagstone terrace that, virtually at the edge of a sharp drop to a private beach, looked out over the waters of Long Island Sound, which now, as the sun set, bordered on blood red.

She had hardly settled when a uniformed butler appeared, stiffly English-formal in dress and manner. Without looking at him, Melissa wordlessly accepted the proffered margarita, pre-sented on a silver tray.

"Anything else, madam?"

"Yes. Tell Grisham I want to see her."

"Miss Grisham has gone for the day, madam."

"She *what?*"

"It's a holiday, madam. She left at noon along

with the two other young office ladies."

Melissa looked at William for the first time, her tone incredulous. "What holiday? I didn't authorize one."

"Veterans Day, madam. Would madam care for anything else?"

A look passed over Melissa's usually expressionless face. It was one of sullen petulance. Making William wait, she stared out over the sound at the far distant shore of Long Island, barely visible in evening's slight haze, before she said, "That will be all, William."

William half bowed, departed as bidden, and Melissa sat in silence, sipping her margarita while letting waves of relief weep over her. Shopping always exhausted her, even if every store, in deference to the money she spent with them, closed its doors to all other customers to ensure her privacy. The soft ring of a gold-plated landline telephone on a glass-topped table by the lounge chair brought her out of her silent reverie.

"Yes?"

A preppy male voice came on. "Melissa? Charles Wheeler. What are you doing home? I thought you had gone to the city."

Melissa made a frowning face and then said, "I'm back, obviously. What do you want?"

"I spoke to your Grisham this morning before she went off, and I understand you are having a party tomorrow."

"You're not calling me about a party. Why?"

"Ah, the sphinx has life today. Well, I can assure you it's not to hear your usual complaints about your chief of staff. Grisham's off-limits on this call. I texted you about the young lady we're sending your way who needs a job at Saugatuck Investments."

"I got it."

"Did you contact your friend Bellistree?"

"Figure it out for yourself. You monitor my landline phone. As well as my cell."

"Melissa, when I ask a simple question, I expect an answer, not any stonewalling bullshit."

The expressionless reclusive suddenly exploded to life. She sat bolt upright angrily and said, "Bullshit yourself, Wheeler. I'm not your office boy. I'm in my home doing you favors."

She was interrupted by his laughter. "No hard feelings, Melissa, but let's get something straight once again. You're not doing me favors. You're doing what you're told to do, which is to inform. You're still the trophy wife of a perverted horror who will probably soon be jailed for life for his predilection for little girls. You got that way when you saw a path from nonentity modeling as Masha Maystrenko, and God only knows what else in Belarus, to big money by accommodating whatever perversion Mr. Nasty had in mind, which I understand to have been legion. One more word from you and you'll find yourself on a return flight to where being Paulstein's trophy doesn't count. Got that? Now down to business."

The brittle reply came only after a long silence. "When does she start?"

"Tomorrow, so be sure you get on to Bellistree right away. When she comes put the young lady up some place. The gardener's cottage if you can't stand the thought of someone lower than you sullying your so-called home. She'll be your way tomorrow, and her name is Gordon. Kelsie Gordon."

There was a click in the receiver of the gold-plated landline phone as Wheeler hung up.

Melisa silently seethed. *And fuck you, Wheeler. I may be a trophy wife, as you put it, you stupid little man, but I know people, and they'll be coming after you one day, and when they do, you won't be laughing.*

Staring out at the sound she fantasized on how he might get what was coming to him, the way her husband had. Wheeler wasn't known as the sex type, but who knew what he did privately, and Melissa enjoyed a silent and ironic laugh at the thought that getting caught screwing around with teenage girls could ruin a man, while men were doing it all over the world and not getting prosecuted for it. Two guys had got her when she was only just thirteen, hadn't they? Paulstein had just been arrogant enough, or stupid enough, more probably, to let himself get caught.

She reached for her cell and texted Bellistree.

Eight

S augatuck Investments occupied an imposing three-story stone building, once a mill that in the nineteenth century manufactured plows and farm tools. Perched right on the banks of the narrow winding Saugatuck River, and only a short distance out of the sizeable town of Westport, its large glass entrance doors beneath an even larger modern glass canopy was in sharp contrast to the otherwise hoary walls and aged appearance of the old mill itself. Imposing in appearance in keeping with its highly respected financial standing, it was arrived at from a parking lot large enough for over fifty cars, which in turn was reached by a low arched stone bridge over the river, leading from a narrow two-lane black top. A score of some twenty offices occupied its interior, along with its kitchen and cafeteria, providing space for over ninety employees.

The Saugatuck Investments president and CEO's office occupied a whole corner of the building. On the third floor, it had a view of a good length of the Saugatuck River to where it rushed over low falls in a spray of white foam and before the river disappeared through the middle of the town of Westport, which it divided on its way before reaching Long Island Sound. The functionality of the softly carpeted office could be seen in a short row of file cabinets against one wall, and on a bookcase occupied by volumes dealing with various aspects of the corporate and financial world. Framed photos of both the president and the vice president of the United States shared some wall space with expensive prints of eighteenth-century full-rigged man-of-war ships doing battle.

Bellistree was a big overweight man with an almost entirely bald head, bulging watery eyes, and a jowly chin that disappeared into a fat neck. Slouching his soft fleshy bulk deep into a high-backed leather chair at his large modern desk, swept clean save for an outbox, a computer monitor, his laptop, and a desk calendar, Bellistree sent a "Not a problem" text back to Melissa. That done, and sinking even deeper in his chair, he enjoyed a certain smug satisfaction.

Wheeler's little FinCen agent was going nowhere. The last thing in the world he wanted was anyone, especially the United States Treasury, moseying around the files of his clients, many of whom were investors with all sorts of personal as well as financial vulnerabilities. Pairing her with a hopeless nerd like Randal Sherman in Research would guarantee she stuck to business. It made no difference if she had experience in research or not. Sherman would be instructed to teach her, and he'd see to it that Karl Fisher, the department head, demanded at least a minimum of information from her that would be guaranteed to tie her down for the foreseeable future. And at the first sign of her doing anything else but research, he'd have an additional talk with Sherman himself and make it very clear that his job depended on finding ways to keep her from doing so.

He'd hardly changed his thinking when a small red light at the base of his landline began to blink repeatedly. It was a secure telephone, the number of which was known to less than a dozen people. Surprised there would be a call at such a near midday hour, Bellistree picked up the receiver.

"Bellistree."

The voice at the other end said, "Mr. Bellistree? This is the office of the vice president. I have Vice President Arthur waiting to speak."

An ardent fly-fisherman, Emanuel Arthur shared his love of the sport with friends and others at Troutlake, his VP getaway home at one of the many trout-stocked lakes in Maine. "Put him on," Bellistree said, at once visualizing the complete isolation of the place, how plainly rustic the small log-built house that was nothing more than a cabin, the absence of any other dwellings around, the silence of the lake, and above all the unusual relative absence of the Secret Service who, at the veep's orders, were kept to a relative few, and those at a distance.

There were vague and indistinguishable mixed voices, and then the vice president came on the line. "Tony?"

"Yes, sir."

"It's Emanuel. How are you?"

"Just fine, sir. And you?"

"The president being pretty incapacitated—that's confidential—so I'm kept pretty busy, but I'll take time for fishing soon. I've got Sokolov flying over to join me. I understand he's a client of yours."

"He is indeed, sir."

"Good, and I hope you'll be able to get up to us too."

"I will, sir, indeed, and look forward to it."

"Did you ever email me the picture you took of that black kid with the whopper he caught?"

"No, sir. But I will, and right away."

"I want Interior to see it and have him tell the parks commissioner to find a way to stop more of his kind from invading the lake. That one came with a whole car full of them. And Tony?"

"Yes, sir."

"If you can arrange our usual lighthearted companionship for Sokolov."

"Not a problem, sir. I'll have a talk with Melissa. She seems to stock a lot of young women at her parties."

"That's Paulstein's trophy woman, right?"

"Yes, sir."

"Good. And nobody older than a hundred, mind you."

Mutual laughter, then, "Tony, on to my finances. How am I doing? I see the market's gone a little crazy this week."

"You're doing fine, sir with your whole blue-chip portfolio. We saw it coming on last month's Dow and the S&P and sold you high. Then when it rebounded, we bought low and watched it leap back up."

"Hedge funds?"

"Your futures we bought leapt high also. You're in the big money, sir."

"That's great, Tony. Until we get to fishing, keep me up to date as usual on any other business. Okay?"

"I certainly will, sir."

The VP rang off, and Bellistree enjoyed a certain smug satisfaction. A few drinks in him at Troutlake and Emanuel Arthur invariably divulged government information or insider deals he picked up from close alliances on Wall Street that proved valuable when it came to his own not inconsiderable investments. Big money was a club where members invariably increased their wealth through association with other members, and the VP was a plus, along with the Russian oil baron Sokolov, who was increasingly investing money in the United States amid visits to further understand how to slowly but favorably turn the American people into an oligarchy of powerful whites who could control the rapid browning of the country and become a valuable Russian ally.

Putting down his own phone, Bellistree realized the VP, and thus, more importantly, Sokolov, didn't know that Treasury had sent down an agent to see how and where Saugatuck Investments was investing, nor, certainly, that he'd taken steps to insure the agent wasn't going anywhere with any information valuable to either the VP or himself. Nor that a highly specialized recorder completely separate from the telephone line had ingested every single word of the conversation they had just had.

The VP would soon be president, no question. The incumbent occupier of the White House was clearly failing fast. And when Emanuel Arthur was President Arthur, he intended to have favors returned when he asked them. The recorder with its revealed racism and attitude favorable to Russia would guarantee that he would.

Nine

Marie Suarez began nearly every day at her desk by watching the earliest news on the TV monitor in her office. She had a long-standing personal rule to keep any political thinking of her own entirely separate from her work.

Recently, however, she was finding this more and more difficult. She kept constantly thinking about the reelection eighteen months ago of a president who had already been revealed, during his first term, as possibly ailing, and now suddenly so ill with an onrushing disease of the pancreas, which the very best of modern medicine seemed unable to check, that the pundits were nearly all agreed he would never finish out the year. Proposed social programs by which he had hoped to lift the burden of extreme poverty from countless millions and other proposals he championed to reverse disastrous manmade climate change had brought sympathetic crowds to their feet, but now seemed sadly doomed by his unfortunate demise.

With his vice president expected soon to be at the helm, the country would be ruled by a man who had campaigned on religious fervor and who had seemed reluctant to support the president he was irrevocably destined to follow. With an ascent to the White House by Emanuel Arthur, many feared that the country would be in the grips of one who had repeatedly shown little if any tolerance for any thoughts or actions that did not fall in line with his devout and ever proselytizing and intolerant Evangelism.

But was there possibly an even more troubling side to the vice president's religiosity, one that could explain an ardent and open embrace of autocrats and oligarchs so contrary to his religious beliefs?

This morning, as spellbound as any, Marie Suarez watched, half-frozen in thought, while in one TV scene after another the vice president chatted with dictators of foreign countries, with his dowdy and adoring wife of forty years on one side, his glamorous daughter Corrina on the other, along with his son, Ellison, whom he'd recently appointed as his principal advisor.

TV cameras caught him on his most recent trip abroad as he warmly shook hands first with the Russian president, a man hardly known for any possible belief in God, then with that thug billionaire, Boris Sokolov, once violently anti-American but now more and more exhibiting a new embrace of anything stamped USA, including vacations there whenever possible.

And here he was again, a moment later, in the Saudi capital, Riyadh, cozying up all smiles to the Saudi prime minister, a man recognized by the whole world as a ruthless despot hardly known for any affinity to Christianity, let alone Evangelism.

That Emanuel Arthur almost certainly would soon occupy the Oval Office did more than give Marie Suarez the shudders; it raised troublesome questions in her mind. What on earth was the VP up to? Why was he even there in the capitals of the most dubious of foreign leaders, relationships with whom at best were based entirely on oil and the sale of armaments? Did the VP's affinity for autocrats, his clear comfort with ruthlessness, blind him to his possibly being used by those very autocrats he'd convinced himself he could manage for America's benefit? What other reason could there be for Putin's close ally, Sokolov, becoming so ardently friendly?

Memory stirred. Long forgotten words were vaguely remembered. Hadn't he once said that "our great nation must remain essentially Nordic," and "It is not only that immigration has to be rigidly controlled, but it should be limited to Europeans who are basically the nature and strength of our country."

They were statements, Marie recalled, that the vice president had made years before he even became a congressman. He'd said them in a speech as class valedictorian at high school graduation when she herself had been one of the graduates. Focusing on the memories now, so many years later, Marie could only note how close those sentiment were to the burgeoning white supremacist nationalism that currently seemed to be everywhere.

A final memory that same year, and before graduation: the VP, along with many other students, herself among them, had once attended a lecture on Russian czars by a visiting historian of note, and she vaguely remembered his rising to ask whether the czars hadn't perhaps been necessary back then as an authoritative and guiding hand to Russia's uncounted mass of peasantry.

Marie suddenly switched off the television in a kind of panic. What on earth was she thinking? Was she crazy? Was she allowing her political revulsion of the vice president to inject itself into professionalism? She pulled herself together. *Emanuel Arthur is neither an autocratic nor a white supremacist, Marie Suarez,* she said to herself. *Cut the fantasy paranoia! He's a God-fearing evangelist happily married to his college sweetheart, which is all anyone has ever accused him of being. At very worst, his cozying up to autocrat adversaries could only mean that in all his naive innocence, he is inadvertently being used for their benefit.*

But in spite of herself, doubts crowded her mind again. The most innocent innocence could be dangerous. It was seven thirty a.m. Staff wouldn't be arriving for another half an hour. She knew, however, that her assistant, Alex

Woodcott, was there. Like her, he invariably came early, usually at six thirty, and somehow, however ferocious the work schedule, he always looked rested, his burly frame and short-cropped graying hair as much a comforting beacon of bureaucratic respectability as the always placid and unworried expression he wore on his pleasantly unfurrowed face. Marie didn't believe in texting or emailing requests to Alex. They'd been working together far too long for such impersonality. He was in the next office, only some dozen feet from hers, and she called out, "Alex?"

He came in, and she said, "Morning."

"Morning, Marie."

"Alex, unofficially and entirely when you find a loose moment or two, could you come up with some travel expenses on the vice president's personal as well as government trips abroad the last five years, with an emphasis on who he saw or telephoned? Besides Putin, whom did he rub elbows with and possibly confide in? Boris Sokolov, for example. He's seeing him soon, I understand, at the VP's Maine hideaway. No rush. Can you manage that?"

"Not a problem." Alex went back to his own office without asking questions. He'd learned not to. Marie ran deep sometimes, kept hunches and totally unconventional ideas to herself. It was the secret of her investigative success.

Ten

Joshua Marshall got to his desk but a few minutes later. He checked out his email and then opened up his file on the month-to-month revenues of most companies that were usually pretty steady, except on rare and well publicized occasions, such as mergers or the introduction of some sensational and well publicized product or service.

While FinCen's agent's job, once at Saugatuck Investments, was to find, through financial investigation, who among all those groups was getting money out of the usual, and who at Saugatuck was sending it to them, his was also to provide additional nonfinancial information as concurring evidence. This he could only do by tracing a number of widely differing public activities of any member of any given group, or the movements of the group itself. It was productive when it came to apparent blossoming of activities in which they were known to invest. This would usually be in talk radio, Facebook ads, Twitter and Instagram, as well as nonfactual reporting and editorials by known local right-wing TV and radio stations and newspapers as well as via local billboards.

Corresponding to this was his file on white supremacists and neo-Nazi militias, along with the horrors many of them were guilty of. Cross-checking from one file to the other, he found himself again worrying about his young colleague's safety. She'd come from the criminal division of the FBI after working for the Brooklyn DA, and yes, she was tough. She'd just proved that. She'd most likely also seen nearly the worst—investigating any Mafia don could be lethal to the investigator—and certainly so in being on the spot at this latest violent killing. Marie Suarez was seldom wrong, he thought, but she might be in this case. Chasing up criminality in financial matters was not the most dangerous work in the world, at least not in most cases. But there was no safe ticket where the filth that were the white supremacists was concerned, and Marie didn't know them the way he did. Their callousness toward their fellow humans almost made the Mafia look saintly, and in an American way matched every cult and religious hatred in history, culminating with the Nazi-inspired Holocaust.

Had Marie made a mistake in not letting the FBI handle this one, instead of sending Agent Gordon to ferret out who was dispensing the Russian laundered money, and precisely to whom? On the surface there could be nothing dangerous at the Saugatuck Investments offices themselves, but the fact that someone in its midst was thought possibly to be helping finance groups like the Colonial Eagles, and the American Defenders of Liberty, along with the infamous Fifty Star bunch, made ferreting around seriously worrying. Any one of those groups harbored calloused killers who were more than capable of risking a quick hit anywhere they felt necessary.

Looking back over the interview the day before, Joshua Marshall found his thoughts straying from that anxiety and down a related but slightly different path. One who often judged others by what he observed in their facial expressions or body language, Joshua found himself reflecting on something he'd noticed in Agent Gordon that had vaguely disturbed him, and which he thought he alone had picked up on. He mentally went back over the lengthy debriefing.

When they'd checked Gordon out on the actual murder, she had shown no particular emotion. Yet then, and to his surprise, twice during their interview with her she'd clearly been swept by strong feelings that showed only fleetingly, and which he was sure neither Marie Suarez nor Charles Wheeler had noticed. At a point when she had responded that she had no problem continuing with the job, she had flushed briefly, almost as though suffused inwardly with anger, even though her response was calm, almost matter-of-fact. Why? And for an instant she'd turned visibly pale when Wheeler had asked her whether if, in her research, she'd picked up anything possibly indicating the vice president's unwitting influence with white supremacy groups.

First emotion on continuing the job, then again where militias and white supremacist groups were concerned. Why? What was she hiding? Had she allowed political or religious sentiments to penetrate her professionalism and possibly jeopardize her job? Or was she possibly two people, one whom they all knew, another whom they didn't know at all except though superficial screening, and who, when working, threw on the icy cold character her colleagues all saw like a disguising cloak?

He personally liked the young woman; everyone at FinCen did. She was attractive, and you couldn't not. But just the same. There was himself, there was Marie, there was Charles, and there was the whole unit to protect. Anger or any other destabilizing emotion could sometimes get out of control and derail an investigation, and there was no use for it in any of their work. She had an impeccable record, but he sensed she'd run into something upsetting to her in this particular case, or that there was something in her private life affecting her personally in some way. When calmly answering their questions, she had exposed to him that there might be, and he determined to find out what it was.

Eleven

A day later in Connecticut and seated in the dark of her rented car, its lights off, Kelsie looked between the tall stone gateposts, the massive wrought-iron gates closed. Far beyond them, at the end of the long gravel driveway, flanked on both sides by beds of flowers and exotic bushes, was the near palatial Paulstein mansion. *Oh, to be so goddamned rich*, she thought.

Twelve hours earlier and back in Washington, she'd been packing a bag and trying to ignore her ever-present worry about Gareth when he asked her how long she'd be gone. He was sober, clearly for the moment off drugs, and she was at least relieved by that. At the same time she had to wonder how long it would last, and was silently praying that it would until she got back.

It seemed only yesterday that she'd had no such worries. Only yesterday, he'd been a little boy vainly clutching at her hand while the minister intoned the immortal words "in sure and certain hope of the resurrection to eternal life," and "ashes to ashes, dust to dust," while they stood at the grave of their mother. Angel, cheeks wet with tears, holding him tight to her, as the coffin was slowly lowered into the grave; and then Angel throwing a handful of symbolic dirt in on it. It was only yesterday that Angel struggled to return things to normal, her to high school, Gareth to kindergarten: Angel taking charge of their lives and being there every morning and every night, Angel loving, counseling, helping, guiding. Until Angel's funeral, and no Angel anymore to protect them both, only herself as Angel's coffin was lowered slowly into the grave, and herself now the one to throw in the handful of dirt while Gareth watched and choked back sobs as she held him tight, as Angel had held her when they'd buried Andrea.

"I don't know how long I'll be gone, Gareth. At least a week. Hopefully not much more. What time today do you see your therapist?"

"Four o'clock."

"Gareth, don't miss it. And tomorrow?"

"Same time."

"As usual, right? So, watch out. I'm going to call you every day. Keep your cell with you. Always."

"How do I reach you?"

"You don't."

"Great. Why the hell not?"

"You know my cell's not private. So maybe only if I locate a secure landline. Perhaps at Saugatuck Investments."

"What's Saugatuck Investments?"

"A hedge fund and investment outfit. I'll have a temporary job with them."

"Doing what? Yeah, same old shit, right? When's the day coming when you loosen up and tell me what you're up to?"

"Gareth, it's government, and I'm not allowed to talk about what I do. You should know that by now, and if you can't accept it, that's your problem. I can't help you with it."

She'd wanted to do something nice for him. To take him out to dinner, maybe with some of his friends, but there hadn't been time. When she'd hugged and kissed him good-bye, he'd looked so forlorn. He always did, ever since Angel had died. Forlorn and seeing her as a mother. She wished he didn't. She wished he'd see her as a sister. He was not a little boy any longer. He was a big six-foot-two hulk now, soon to graduate university and go on to medical school, probably screwing every girl he could get his hands on. Maybe one of them one day would help him with his addiction problem. Girls were a lot brighter and far more confident than when she was in college. A lot of them really took things in hand.

Leaving home and Gareth, she'd gone straight to a meeting with Charles Wheeler in an inconspicuous corner of the VIP lounge at Reagan National Airport. There, looking for all the world like a couple perhaps off on a vacation, and virtually out of sight or sound of anyone who could conceivably matter, he'd briefed her on the next phase of her job.

She hadn't minded the factual statistics; they were necessary, but she'd hated his rather imperious manner, as though he considered himself her handler. As if she needed one. Or ever had in the long six months on the job that had finally brought her to what everybody, including herself, saw as nearing a critical end.

Happy finally to be rid of Wheeler, she'd boarded the flight from Washington to LaGuardia in New York, and taken a train from Grand Central Station to her final destination, which was Westport, Connecticut, and there rented a car right at the station. She'd decided that rather than immediately cope with Mrs. Paulstein, she'd wait until the next day, and she had checked into a convenient hotel, then had taken time to size up the lay of the land around town. She'd memorized the relatively simplistic street system and had driven a quarter mile out through a poorer area of suburbs, where little and mostly white clapboarded ranch-style houses were set on one-eighth-acre well-tended plots.

When the suburbs ended, she'd followed the narrow swift-moving Saugatuck River through woods to Saugatuck Investments' big stone building. There, she'd parked and entered the lobby through the glass entrance doors to take a good look at the board listing the different departments, while avoiding as best she could the questioning of her presence by both the doorman and the smartly tailored young receptionist, who sat authoritatively behind a strategically placed desk. *Swank joint,* she'd thought, *all tailored to show clients total respectability. Well, Mr. Bellistree and or whomever, I'm here to see just how respectable you actually are.*

From trying to calm Gareth back home, meeting Wheeler at the airport, and then coming to Westport, it had been an exceptionally long day. Now, with her busy afternoon finally behind her, and still parked by the gates shielding the world from the driveway and Soundview, she got out her cell and, again feeling disbelief, played the recording she'd made of Wheeler's instructions at their Reagan National meeting.

Looking around the VIP lounge as though they were being spied on by the occasional passerby going to the restrooms or headed to the bar for another drink, Wheeler had objected to her obvious recording of their talk. He'd said angrily, "I don't like being taped."

"Well, swallow it." She'd been deliberately cold and unpleasant. Right from the moment they'd met. Something about his ridiculous bow tie and preppy Ivy League manner irked. And there was more: he came across to her as two-faced. But two-faced about what, she couldn't figure. She'd said, "Do you want me to fuck up because I couldn't remember one of your golden instructions? Or should I more accurately say, your rather obnoxiously put orders?"

She'd erased further instructions but not the look of fury that took over his face. He'd started off with the obvious, as if she didn't know. He'd said, "You'll need a job at Saugatuck, and we're giving you a contact to arrange employment for you there as soon as possible."

Herself, only one word, and abruptly: "Who?"

Him: "Someone who will rather surprise you. You've heard of Herbert Paulstein?"

"Of course," and she'd thought, *Jesus, who hadn't?* The multibillionaire had been headlines for the past six months when he'd been finally exposed in his sordid abuse for years of women and underage girls. Saugatuck Investments had once been part of his financial empire, along with half a dozen other similar financial organizations he owned. More privately than the famous twenty-bedroom Soundview, in an exclusively wealthy area of Westport, where he had long and actively entertained famed Hollywood celebrities as well as leading political figures, he boasted a hundred-and-fifty-foot yacht, a private Boeing 737, a luxury home in the Caribbean, and an apartment in Paris.

"Your contact at Westport will be with his soon to be ex-wife."

She'd been caught off-guard by this, and now stared, as she had at Wheeler, in total disbelief at her cell phone as it rolled out his words all over again, along with her startled responses. Seated in the dark security of her rented car, she pictured the incredibly beautiful fashion-perfect and expressionless famed young wife who was so shy of the public as to be seen as a virtual recluse. Reclusively guarded or vacuously empty? she wondered. Some thought one thing, others differently, while in spite of endless press coverage, she had somehow miraculously managed to keep herself respectably separate from the sickening image of her husband.

Unable when meeting Wheeler to maintain the icy coldness she'd deliberately imposed on him, Kelsie had burst out laughing. "Melissa Paulstein? You have to be kidding."

"I kid thee not," Wheeler said, his tone betraying the same suspicious dislike for her that she held for him. "I speak of the tabloid-shy mystery wife who clearly could only have married a pig like Paulstein for money. I know it sounds insane, but she's in our pocket."

It was an equally startling revelation, one that instantly raised the question: In FinCen's pocket? How come? Why? What had the famous woman, clearly considered isolated and in no way responsible for the appalling behavior and disgrace of her husband, done to make herself vulnerable? Kelsie said, "And what's our leverage?"

Wheeler had assumed a smug and condescending tone, as though getting real pleasure from his revelation. He said, "With her forthcoming divorce from Paulstein, someone at Homeland Security's ICE, whom her husband had stepped on once too often, began a revenge questioning of irregularities in her green card. What was a nobody nude model from Belarus doing here? So, we made a deal. If she spilled beans not just about her husband's illicit finances but also on the current doings of his many financier friends who still flock around her like moths around a bright light, we'd see to it that ICE laid off. She was only too happy to cooperate because she's said a lot of insulting things about the dictator in Belarus when Paulstein was riding high. Back there, her life wouldn't be worth a nickel."

"Okay, got it, the leverage. But what does it produce for us?"

"Among Paulstein's cronies, whom she continues to entertain, could well be some familiar with and possibly getting the money transfers you've been tracking. Marshall thinks there might be as many as four, all suspected white nationalists he'd especially like to know about who are hiding behind corporate respectability while secretly representing or running hate groups. Alcohol, especially champagne, flows like water at Melissa's parties, giving her a good shot at picking up any unintentional revelations."

Kelsie clicked off the audio on her cell, put the car in gear, and headed back to the hotel where she'd checked in that morning. The Paulstein woman was having a dinner party the next night, Wheeler had told her, and one of the guests would be Anthony Bellistree, the president and CEO of Saugatuck Investments. It was pretty clear, Wheeler said, that he was close to, if not intimate, with Melissa.

"Who knows, given her background back in

Belarus before she married Paulstein," Wheeler said, with an insinuating laugh. "Her connection with him, other than her husband and herself being his clients, will get you a job at Saugatuck."

Kelsie hadn't wanted to hear more, and had told him so. After he'd left her to herself and her flight to New York, she'd muttered, "Shit," and had gone to the bar in the VIP lounge for another vodka. She would have preferred being involved with some of the Mafia she'd run into while working in Brooklyn than with anyone in the spoiled rich billionaire crowd.

They had been a truly rough bunch, and memory of them was to Kelsie as vivid today as when she'd brought them to justice. One of her first assignments was to check out Alfonso Bertucci, the famous don of the Bertucci family, by listing all court documents in suits he'd been involved in over the past ten years, along with all newspaper and other publicity items, no matter how small and insignificant they had seemed.

She had gone a very large step farther without telling the DA for fear he'd pull her from the case. Through a cooperative employment agency that owed the DA one, she'd posed as an illiterate Finnish cleaning woman, fresh off the boat, and had secured a job at the don's home in Brooklyn, doing the heavy cleaning his regular staff didn't like to do—mopping filthy basement floors, cleaning toilets and ovens, and anything else that put her on her hands and knees with a pail of filthy water and a scrub brush while looking like she was grateful for the job.

Once well into the work, with the family accustomed to her silent presence, she'd worn a wire and had recorded several conversations between the don and some of his shadier gang members, who carried out his far less than legal orders, including disposing of people the don found in his way.

Her job with Don Bertucci came to an abrupt end when she had surrendered the wire with its many damming recordings to a judge at the trial of Michael Donato, owner of a small tire sales shop accused of a murder, which clearly was shown on the wire as having been ordered by Don Bertucci and carried out by Carlos, one of his hit men. Mike Donato had escaped the death penalty and had gone free to return to his tire shop. But her action in publicly revealing her undercover role had raised legal questions about the wire that had caused the DA serious problems, and herself her job when her irate boss summarily fired her.

Back in her hotel room in Westport, and as she got ready for bed, she clicked on CNN. The news was still speculating about the "whistle-blower shooting," and there was more about her—the girl in the floppy blue hat—Who was she?—than about the murder itself, or about Prince Mohammed Adi. She got on the hotel phone to Gareth. And when he answered, she realized to her relief that he'd been asleep. She'd forgotten how late it was. Her traveling bedside clock's luminous red figures said 12:05.

"Sorry to wake you."

"Okay."

"How was your day?"

"We won our game against Georgetown."

"Lacrosse?"

"Yeah. Beat them silly."

"Final exams on the way, right?"

"I've already done half of them. Aced one, I'm sure."

"Great. Keep it up and go back to sleep on it. Love you."

"Love you too."

A phone click and then silence. Kelsie turned off her light, and tried not to think of the next day or let it crowd out her relief that Gareth was sober and for the moment free of drugs.

Twelve

The research division of Saugatuck Investments was in a section of its own. Located on the second floor of the company's big three-story building, it was occupied by a dozen people skilled in understanding corporate structure, business competition, and a wide variety of industries and product markets. Their job was to study and analyze every aspect of corporations considered a possible good risk for investment capital and report their recommendation to invest or not to invest to the head office.

At mid-morning coffee break, researchers, who occupied the cubicles in which each did his or her work, pushed away from the computers and laptops set on the wide shelving that wrapped around each cubicle's three sides. The break, besides a sudden uproar of chatter that shattered the otherwise stillness of the room, meant indulging in coffee, muffins, and fruit smoothies. These welcome and unpaid-for treats were picked from a trolley rolled into their area by a uniformed employee from the company cafeteria on the ground floor, and perhaps served to emphasize that Saugatuck Investments was a good place to work. Salaries were above average, pension benefits were generous, and health care was largely paid for, along with vacations. A registered nurse offered advice and treated minor problems in a well-stocked clinic on the ground floor. There was liberal maternity leave for those starting in on parenthood, and above all there was Saugatuck Investments' reputation, which was one of success as well as eminent respectability in a business where, more often than not, there was more than a hint of shady dealings. Employees took pride in working there.

One of the researchers in the research department was a young man named Randal Sherman. Tall, on the thin side, his tousled hair always an uncombed mess, his blandly expressionless eyes forever peered over the top of large black-rimmed glasses. He had little if any interest in pop culture or in office get-togethers or inter-department sporting events. At boisterous, noisy office parties where they all drank too much, he stood off by himself, unable to join in the fun. In short, he seemed to his coworkers as stand-offish, even hostile, and so many avoided him as much as possible.

Randal in turn had as little use for his fellow researchers as they had for him. To him they were, for the most part, as far removed from his thinking, his background, and his home life as aliens. San Francisco–raised, his mother played the violin in a symphony orchestra, and his father was a doctor. A bookworm, he was a devotee of classical music.

He had done his best to make his work space habitable. His computer monitor and keyboard took up half the broad wrap-around shelf that served as a desk; his laptop and a stack of files the other. On the glass upper wall of his cubicle, he'd pasted up countryside pictures—mountains, the seaside, pastures, and one of his parents.

There was an interoffice phone he rarely used—all interoffice communication was largely by email or texting, and outside communication generally frowned upon unless due to some sort of emergency. There were two file cabinets under the shelf, and a large television screen on the room's far wall, available to all, was daily tuned to a financial channel offering up-to-the-minute graphs, charts, and news on the U.S. economy as well as the stock markets in the U.S., London, Tokyo, Sydney, and Beijing.

Always curious about anything and everything, something both his parents had readily fostered, he'd insisted after college at Berkeley on setting out on his own in life, and had tried a number of jobs where what they were doing he found exciting. He'd worked at an experimental chemical lab looking into what the lab claimed as "new worlds." At another job he delved into ways of increasing crop growth through deep ploughing, better organized irrigation, and the use of composted organic fertilizer. When he became interested in progress in the development of new ways of manufacturing, he'd decided to spend some time in researching business and industry. Saugatuck Investments had seemed a good place to start. They had to clearly understand companies and their future in order to invest in them, and he'd applied for a job, had been accepted, and to date had found the work highly interesting.

Randal was something of a computer whiz, and endless internet research had always been to him like playing detective. Saugatuck Investments provided new fields for his curiosity. Profiling a specific company that had requested serious investment, and issuing an accurate report detailing every possible aspect of the company's current and future operations, as well as similar projections of its leading competitors—all that was right up his alley.

He was disappointed in the investment firm's atmosphere, however. He found it restrictive and depressing. He especially disliked the president and CEO, Anthony Bellistree. He thought him an arrogant bully and suspected, from the odd remark Bellistree threw out, that he was secretly a bigot, even a white supremacist.

But a job was a job. He had charted a course in life in which he was determined to be self-sufficient, and especially to be of financial help to his parents, if needed, when they had both ceased working and their income was considerably reduced. It wouldn't do in searching out some future job to not show that he'd stuck this one for at least a respectable amount of time.

Deep in an analysis of short-range air transport competition faced by a budding new local airline, he was startled to find none other than the bulky, slouching, and unattractive presence of Bellistree himself when the CEO appeared unannounced at his cubicle.

"Randal, drop what you are doing. I need your attention."

"Sir?"

"We are taking on a new researcher."

"Yes, sir."

"She'll be occupying the space next to yours. We're moving out the party currently there in order to accommodate."

"Yes, sir."

Randal's thoughts moved quickly from jet aircraft to the space next to him. Currently it was occupied by Esther Small, an older woman who made no attempt to hide her general disapproval of him. He was instantly swept by a feeling of delight that she'd be gone as well as curiosity about what the new occupier would be like.

Bellistree again, his voice authority without mercy. "We will expect you to get her started. Familiarize her with us and the job the first few days, and answer any questions she might have. Then if she's not already a skilled researcher, teach her what she needs to know and do on the job. Do I make myself clear?"

"Yes, sir."

Then, as silently as he'd come, Bellistree was gone, leaving Randal wondering. People came and went in research. Nothing dramatic about that, but it was always Karl Fisher, the lank balding department manager, who, with his usual sour expression that matched his bad breath, announced any change. Why today Bellistree himself?

His appearance left Randal, besides with annoyance at his boss's arrogant tone, also wondering why he of all people was to be stuck with hosting a new researcher. Familiarize her with us, get her started? Well, okay, sure, but why him? Why not someone else? Why was she so important as to evacuate the cubicle next to his for her? There were two cubicles nearer to the door that had been unoccupied for weeks.

After a while he stopped asking questions and went back to studying the competition of the proposed new airline company.

Thirteen

At around eleven the same day, Melissa was again on the terrace at Soundview. She was having breakfast, served up on a tray with coffee along with a second bloody mary, and the day, already rapidly approaching the noon hour, was already hot and windless. A sun like burnished brass and long above the horizon mercilessly glared at her off the glassily smooth water of the sound as well as off the glass-topped table occupied in part by her breakfast tray. She wore dark glasses and was fighting a hangover. Kicking herself for drinking too much the night before, she tried to pull herself together and organize her day before she bathed and dressed for the evening.

Grisham had made all the arrangements for drinks, dinner and after-dinner coffee, and more drinks. She'd done everything the day before, and as always, right down to the last flower in the extensive floral arrangements. She'd chosen with William the several different kinds of vintage wine, and carefully plotted the complex seating arrangement—who to put next to whom—at each of the dozen tables that would occupy the large paneled dining room. She'd also discussed and ordered the menu from aperitif to desert with Riccard, the French chef Paulstein had imported ten years ago. Grisham was paid a lot, but she was worth it. She hailed from a socially prominent family, and in previous employment with people new to money and refinement of any sort, had shown expertise in all of it.

Melissa's thoughts about the evening were interrupted by the insistent voice of the maid. "Madam … madam …"

Turning her head only enough to catch a glimpse of starched white uniform, Melissa said, "Yes? What is it?" She could never remember the maid's name, and although there for as long as she could remember, she kept getting her mixed up with one of the two upstairs ones as well as the other one downstairs.

"There's lady at the door, madam. She says she's been sent from Washington to see you."

"Washington?" And then Melissa remembered. Yesterday when that awful scum Wheeler had called, he'd also told her she had to make a room available for some woman, and it had to be the one at the door, who else. She wasn't expecting anybody. Instant anger flared up through her whole being, and her head lanced pain worse than ever. Having one of Wheeler's agents settled on her was the last thing she wanted. Mentally, she added it to a list of other Wheeler demands she'd reckon with when her day came.

"Oh, for Chrissake, send her in."

"Yes, madam."

The maid departed and at the front door found Kelsie still waiting. "Madam will see you now," she said. Without asking, she seized the pull handle of Kelsie's wheeled suitcase. "If you'd be so good, miss, as to follow me, madam is on the terrace."

Was there a hint of carefully suppressed resentment in the maid's tone? Kelsie was sure she'd caught at least a touch of it, which might foretell what she could expect when she met "madam" herself. And then something like *Holy smoke, is this for real?* was her next thought as she caught her first wide glimpse of the wealth displayed in the front hall, the marble floor, the huge gilded chandeliers whose dozens of lights dazzlingly reflected from scores of delicately hung crystals surrounding them, the expensive modern seascapes decorating the wall of a wide and sinewy double stair that stretched upward.

Equally dazzling was the living room as they crossed it, footsteps muffled to near silence by its thickly woven carpet graced by expensive designer furniture that was almost dwarfed, along with a Steinway grand, by the room's daylight-flooded size.

But Kelsie, although she thought she ought to be, wasn't impressed. She couldn't help compare all of it to her own shabby little house and those of all her neighbors in Lincoln Park, and felt, instead of awe or even any lesser appreciation, a renewed wave of the irritation she'd experienced driving up the long gravel driveway through a carefully landscaped area of decorative and exotic trees and bushes before confronted by the massive two-story stone bulk of the house itself. First one couple and now just one woman living in a house built for twenty people or more? Paulstein, she'd remembered, had fled pretrial, and while on a twenty-million-dollar bond, to a country that had no extradition treaty with the USA.

She was even less impressed, when reaching the terrace, with her first sight of the famed inscrutable model who had married the finance mogul. Still in a designer house coat that when opened revealed expensive silk pajamas, Melissa managed to turn in her chair at the glass-topped breakfast table with a pretense of not knowing why the young woman who stood looking down at her was there.

"Yes? You wanted to see me?"

Kelsie quickly caught onto the act. *Clever bitch*, she thought, and decided not to play along with it. She trusted the team back in Washington, especially Wheeler, to have judged the woman accurately.

She said coldly, "Yes, and I think you know why I am here, Mrs. Paulstein. FinCen, that's the United States Treasury Department, if you can't remember, has set me up to stay with you and for your immediate influence in getting me employment at Saugatuck Investments. I understand you are close, maybe even intimate, with the guy who runs the place, one Anthony Bellistree?"

It worked. Melissa stiffened, pulling her house coat close round her pajamas, and took a first good look at the unexpected and unwanted interloper. She saw a well-dressed person a little older than herself, and one who had about her the business appearance and no-nonsense air of officialdom. She fixed Kelsie with a hostile stare.

"I see you've been briefed, so we don't need to stand on ceremony. I've already spoken to Mr. Bellistree, who runs Saugatuck, and a job at Saugatuck, I'm sure, will await you." She stared coldly at Kelsie and turned to the maid who, not yet departed, awaited orders, mouth agape at what she'd just heard.

"You. What's your name?"

"Agnes, madam."

"Ah, yes. Show Miss Gordon to one of the guest rooms in the south wing." And to Kelsie, "If you need anything, Agnes will accommodate you." Then, dismissively pouring coffee into a Wedgwood china coffee cup, Melissa turned away from both Kelsie and the maid.

Kelsie wasn't having it and once more brought Melissa up sharply. She said, "Saugatuck Investments? When?" And said nothing further, and waited.

Melissa turned again, stared at Kelsie, expressionless, a painfully long and silent moment to cover the rage she felt at such insolence, and then said, "Tony Bellistree will be here tonight at a dinner I'm giving. You can ask him beforehand. I'll have Grisham let you know when he arrives."

"And before *he* dines," Kelsie thought. *Okay, the kitchen for me, which might be more fun.* Aloud, and returning Melissa's icy look, she said, "Thank you. I'll plan to do just that."

When she'd gone with Agnes, Melissa lay back, swallowing her fury at what she saw as hostility, and was glad she'd assigned the unwanted woman a room as far away as possible. That she'd be somewhat at hand, possibly, that evening because of her meeting Bellistree was about all she could bear to put up with.

She hadn't allowed herself much more than a glance, but the young woman had a look she'd early on in Belarus got used to, and now especially in America. It wasn't just one of unbending officialdom. This was a little miss smart-ass, never-give-up, typical cop type, and she was going to have to be careful until the chance came along to get rid of her. This woman wasn't Wheeler, whom she could wrap around her little finger, and who thought he was using her at will when he was using her only when it suited her. She had bigger fish to fry than cooperating with the U.S. Treasury and its stupid democratic-minded bureaucrats, think what they would.

Her thoughts were interrupted by a deeply-strong Russian-accented male voice. "Good morning, Mrs. Paulstein."

The greeting was punctuated by a low and slightly amused laugh. Startled, Melissa turned and looked up, only remembering as she did the man's presence from the day before and the evening they had spent together over margaritas for her and scotch for him after a dinner for two for which she had given special orders to the chef imported from Paris by her husband.

"Boris!"

"Melissa!" Boris Sokolov laughed again and as Melissa moved slightly to accommodate him, and sat familiarly down by her side on the chaise longue. He was a tall, powerful man, hair barely graying, with a classically strong Russian face displaying white, perfectly even teeth in a firm jaw, and his muscular bronzed torso not fully covered by a terry-cloth robe that was on the small side.

Melissa said, "You startled me. I thought from what you said last night that you'd be gone already."

"To see Bellistree? Yes. I'd planned to go to his little banking company, Sauga something or whatever he calls it, this morning."

"Saugatuck Investments, and it's not so little."

"Of course, but I changed my mind somewhere between midnight and two a.m." Sokolov rested one big hand on her thigh.

Melissa laughed. It was on her tongue to say, "I wonder why." Boris Sokolov had spent those hours in her bed, but she said nothing and waited.

"Since I remember you are giving a party tonight, and Bellistree will be a guest, I decided to wait out the day."

Melissa smiled. She'd hooked him, at least temporarily, and for the sake of being pleasant in their business. Nobody, she knew, ever hooked Boris Sokolov permanently. He was too smart, too one step ahead.

"We need to talk," he said.

"I'm listening. I had breakfast sent to your room, and I'm sure there was coffee with it. Would you like more, or would you prefer a scotch?"

"Thank you. Yes, a scotch."

"What was it you wanted to talk about?"

"I just want to be clear on where we are. This little girl I saw through my window come up in an old car. Is this the agent Wheeler is sending down? She's now gone off to her room or somewhere else?"

"Yes." Melissa reached to pointedly cut a switch on a small panel by her telephone. "So we can't heard by Grisham."

He nodded, looked around, and said, Russian accent thick, "Our deal, then. My part, I shut up your tin-pot Belarus dictator permanently where you are concerned in case you should ever go back, and here, also, if he should be so foolish as to stretch a long arm after you. Your part," he continued, "You keep a very close eye on Wheeler's young woman and report to me who she sees, where she goes, and how much spying-around progress she makes. Do I make myself heard? I need to know when she becomes expendable."

Melissa studied him. When Boris Sokolov wasn't talking business, he was often laughing, his green-gray eyes dancing with amusement. They weren't dancing now.

"Very clear," she said. She was glad he was going to wait to see Bellistree until evening. It meant he would have a whole afternoon with little to do. She rested a jeweled hand on his. She'd see to it that he wasn't bored.

Fourteen

That same morning saw a man sitting across her cluttered desk from Marie Suarez in her barren FinCen office. He had one of those well-shaven faces that was unidentifiable in its very ordinariness. The same could be said for his modestly subdued tie, his shirt and immaculately pressed business suit, even his high-polished shoes and dark socks. None of it would call favorable attention, nor in an opposite sense any sort of disapproval. There was something about his entire and otherwise rather pleasant being that was Washington DC anonymity. Even his name—Jim Thorpe. Those facts suited him fine. He was an agent for the FBI, one of a team working in counterintelligence.

Marie had coffee brought in from the Starbucks around the corner, and after very brief pleasantries, Thorpe at once proceeded to tell her the reason why he'd phoned the day before requesting a few minutes of her time. About what, he hadn't said when he'd called, except that he'd explain when he saw her. She didn't know him, but he was not someone she could refuse, and his request had kept her awake a while during the night, racking her mind as to what possibly he'd have to say. She had a department of more than twenty under her, and as far as she knew, they had all passed extensive checks before being hired. She even knew some of them personally, was aware of their lives away from work and any problems they might have with family or finance. She could think of nothing.

Could it have been something political she herself might have said somewhere at sometime? She always tried and was successful, she hoped, to keep any discussion, even any thought of politics or personal opinions, away from her professional and office life, and she asked the same from all who worked for her. Privately, though, she had plenty of thoughts and opinions. She barely tolerated the ancient and ailing president and thoroughly detested the devoutly religious vice president, soon to follow him into the White House.

Her worried thoughts were interrupted by her visitor. He put down his coffee mug, briefly collected his own thoughts, and then said, "We think there's possibly a leak in your department."

It was abrupt and unexpected, and Marie managed to hide that she was completely taken back. She said, "Oh?" And for a moment couldn't think of anything else to say.

"No cause for immediate alarm. I said possibly, right? You have someone up in Connecticut at the Saugatuck Investment Company, I believe. That's a well-known hedge fund group."

"Yes, we do."

"One Kelsie Gordon?"

"Yes."

Marie's instant concern, however, was then replaced by an equally instant wave of relief when her FBI visitor said, "It's not her, however. We know Agent Gordon and still see her as one of us. We're more concerned with her immediate handler, if you can call him that."

"Charles Wheeler?" Marie didn't try to hide her surprise.

"He has frequent exchanges with Melissa Paulstein."

"Well, yes, Charles does. But that's part of his job. We're using Paulstein. But not without her complete compliance, I hasten to add. She regularly holds parties for leading banker friends of her husband. Her guests also include suspected white nationalists, some even of neo-Nazism and possible recipients of laundered money we've traced. She is personally close to Bellistree, the CEO of Saugatuck Investments, who buddies with both the VP and Boris Sokolov and who, incidentally, we also suspect of white supremacy. The Paulstein woman via Charles was able to quickly get Bellistree to agree to our plant there, and we expect that to soon pay off in a flow of encrypted information from Miss Gordon."

The FBI agent remained expressionless, showing relatively little interest in what she had said. "We look forward to Gordon's final report. Possible leakage via Charles Wheeler is only just that—possible. It won't be defined or negated completely until we can ascertain the meaning of some of the—shall I call them asides?—in emails between him and Mrs. Paulstein."

"Could you give me an example, Mr. Thorpe?"

Thorpe unfolded a note sheet he took from his pocket. "In an email he sent her on the 15th, he said, 'Please report to me by return if Gordon correctly placed.' Then he added, 'And don't forget that *extra you promised.*'"

Thorpe continued, "In an email a day later, he wrote, 'Send me Bellistree's affirmation that the plant went well. And send me info *on our other agreement.*' Thorpe lowered the paper. "What 'extra' was promised, and what is meant by 'our other agreement'? We find both phrases out of context with the main message. It's as though he had an entirely different affair going other than planting Miss Gordon."

Maria was too much a veteran to allow herself to be thrown off balance by what she heard, and something about the authoritative self-assurance of the FBI agent raised her hackles. She said, "Charles has a very unconventional— might I say freewheeling—way of handling things. He had to develop a trusting relation-ship with Mrs. Paulstein before he could enlist her help in planting Gordon. I suggest you meet with him and discuss the connection."

"That's your job, Miss Suarez," Thorpe replied rather coldly. "You're his boss. Wheeler's basic integrity isn't yet being questioned. My job is only to alert you as department head that there could be a problem with him where discretion is concerned."

"Of course."

"I'm sure you will advise Agent Gordon to mind her step with anything that might arise in her further work. We don't want the White House up in arms for whatever reason." Thorpe rose. "I appreciate your time." He dropped his card on Suarez's desk. "Keep me informed as to your talk with Wheeler. We will continue to closely monitor his communications. And let us know whatever Gordon might pick up on the way about the Saugatuck CEO, and if she picks up on when he next plans visiting the VP's fishing hideaway at Troutlake in Maine the same time as the VP does." He smiled for the first time. "Lot more drinking than fishing, the Secret Service tells me."

"The VP drinking?"

"Yeah, drinking and the dubious company that often goes with it. I know, he's devout evangelical and all that, but just the same, he sometimes gives the Secret Service boys a real headache. He demands privacy, and he's never happy when they accompany him up there. He insists their unit be so reduced as to be ridiculous. They couldn't stop anyone from walking right into the luxe cabin he had constructed for himself." Jim Thorpe shrugged and added, "Takes all kinds, I guess. So again, tell your Miss Gordon to tread carefully. We don't want anything revealed that we can't put a lid on before the press chances to get hold of it."

When he had gone, Marie spent quite a few minutes thinking about his revelations. Hearing them, she'd been careful not to expose certain misgivings she herself had about Charles Wheeler. Her thoughts went back over various talks she'd had with him about Melissa. There'd been nothing untoward in anything he'd said. Or had there been? Now she asked herself if she had once or twice not felt or noticed that he seemed to know Melissa in a way other than professional when discussing the connection he was making with her?

Nothing had been said that would indicate so. But what about attitude? She tried to relive the conversations she'd had with him when he'd first suggested using Melissa Paulstein. She'd been told how he'd had the chance to meet her when he took advantage of an invitation to one of Paulstein's famous celebrity parties, courtesy of a college classmate who was in with her; how he'd come to talk to her very briefly in the alcoholic swirl of the party; how he'd used that briefest of social meetings to take a chance and call on her after her husband's arrest and removal, and in several subsequent meetings lay his cards bluntly on the table.

All very candid. Perhaps too much so? Had there been something else? Anything? Or nothing? Was she imagining a vague troubled feeling that how he'd hooked Melissa Paulstein was just a little *too* good?

Suarez realized that like it or not, she had to think about it further, perhaps entice Charles into a longer explanation of how he'd come to use Melissa, and this time to listen more carefully to pick up any suspicious nuance, if she detected any. And above all, to keep a very close eye on him. Even though she didn't much like Thorpe, or ever giving ground to the FBI, few in the bureau were fools, and certainly Thorpe hadn't given her the impression that he was.

Resolving to stay in close connection with him, she went back to doing what she'd been doing when interrupted, reviewing the expense figures on Vice President Arthur's Russian forays that Alex had left on her desk and which she'd been deep into before the appearance of the FBI agent Jim Thorpe.

Several items struck her as unusual. The Veep had indulged, at taxpayer expense, in two unscheduled and press-free side trips to a well-known resort on the Black Sea where Boris Sokolov had a luxurious summer home. There'd been no hotel or any other expenses listed other than the Air Force flights there and back, and those related to a limited number of Secret Service agents, and she could not escape the conclusion that Arthur had possibly stayed with Sokolov who later, according to Kelsie Gordon and FinCen's embassy-based Russian operators, had transferred a very large sum of money from one of the oligarch billionaire's corporate accounts to a central Russian bank in Moscow.

Could this be the money, as stated by both Gordon and Mohammed Adi, that finally ended up with Saugatuck Investments? Two visits, and a highly suspect money transfer, could the vice president have innocently or even plain stupidly revealed something, anything, that made the transference of large sums from Russia to the USA especially attractive? And worse, laid himself open to possible blackmail once he was in the Oval Office? Excessive religiosity could blind a person to reality.

A red flag was suddenly raised in Marie's mind. For a moment, it erased her discomfort over Wheeler's strange email exchanges.

She made some notes to herself and then, her eye falling on the card the FBI's Thorpe had left on her desk, she sent a coded text message to Kelsie Gordon, instructing her until further notice to make her daily reports as well as any other communication to her direct and not to Wheeler.

Fifteen

When shown to her room down at the end of an endlessly long upstairs corridor in what Melissa had said was the south wing, Kelsie's thoughts jumbled. She wished Suarez could have been the one handling Melissa and not Wheeler. It took a woman to know one, she thought. Men were easily deceived, and something about Melissa jarred. She had at once sensed there was more to the famed trophy wife than appeared, and Suarez would have been better than Wheeler, she felt certain, at ferreting out what lay behind the inscrutable mask of the model, who in Belarus had been Masha Maystrenko, besides using her marriage to a disgraced husband for everything she could get out of it. Suarez might possibly see more that Melissa might be keeping out of sight and to herself.

For it took something, Kelsie thought, besides a pretty face, seductive female wiles, and a willing to bed anybody with wealth to nail a notorious reprobate and womanizer like Paulstein. Monstrous though he was, he wasn't after all any less stupid about women than most billionaires. It took something far deeper than a quick screw with the guy to get him to the altar. It took a kind of clever deviousness, the ability to utterly and believably present yourself as one sort of woman while actually being someone quite different.

She was going, Kelsie thought, to have to keep a wary eye on Melissa. Wheeler might have seriously underestimated Paulstein's wife, whom she was certain might be someone far from the indolent pajamaed lady at a noon-time breakfast to whom she'd just been introduced. She could be playing some sort of double game Wheeler hadn't yet cottoned onto, although what that game might be and to what aim, at the moment she had no idea.

Kelsie thought that the guest room assigned to her befitted the palatial character of Soundview. It was a suite—two rooms, one a bedroom, the other a lounge pleasantly decorated with cream-colored couches, chairs, and a desk outfitted with a laptop along with a copier and a printer which, if wanted, was pulled out from a handsome cabinet built to compliment the French provincial decor of the suite.

On first entering, she guessed its choice out of the twenty-odd rooms available had been the maid's who escorted her to it. She had made an effort to counter Melissa's rude order to the crisply uniformed young woman. She had chatted pleasantly and thanked her profusely for toting about her suitcase, and had been relieved to see her resentful silence slowly fade as she showed off the various beneficial aspects of the suite. The previous occupant had been a well-known movie star, she said, who had come with an entourage of her own: a servant and several little dogs. Becoming talkative, she'd added, "Most guests were nice and tipped a lot. But we get one who only comes once in a while. He's awful ugly and has no manners and talks some funny language with madam."

Before coming, Kelsie had been warned that besides every kind of electronic surveillance at Soundview, there were hidden cameras everywhere to record visually every happening. That she might be constantly watched by somebody was chilling. Who? Melissa? It hadn't made sense, but alarm bells rang and she cast anxiously around the room to see if she could find any hidden cameras. Finding nothing, however, she made up her mind that she'd confront Melissa the next day and demand that any observation must cease at once. She was sure she'd know if Melissa was lying or not if Melissa denied any knowledge of camera scrutiny.

Then, waiting out the day until shortly before evening, when certain Melissa would be getting ready for dinner, she went directly down a back stair to the dining room, avoiding Grisham, who, satisfied all arrangements were perfect, was in her office.

There were six tables, each seating eight

and, as expected, all were carefully set for diner: crystal glassware, silver cutlery, and Wedgewood china dinner plates marked a place at each table for each guest. Knowing she might be on camera and carefully shielding her cell from sight, Kelsie quickly took shots of every one of the place cards that she saw, their names clearly written in flowery script. She'd chosen her moment right. Passing through the library when heading back to her room upstairs, she only just avoided Grisham returning to the dining room to make sure, in a last inspection, that all was perfect.

Regaining her room, and prepared to email the photos to Wheeler, she was surprised to find Suarez's order that she report to her instead. Why? She could find no answer, but found herself relieved. Wheeler's bonhomie Ivy League responses had started to irritate her. Sometimes he seemed to deliberately avoid answering a question, and she had begun to feel certain that he wasn't taking her reports seriously.

After sending off the photos to Suarez along with her full report, she was greeted by noise from the parking lot, laughter and cries of greeting, indicating that guests were beginning to arrive, and she prepared to go back downstairs. She freshened up, redid her makeup, and changed out of street clothes into a basic black sheath she had found so useful in all the European Embassy affairs she'd attended. Then, after adding her only jewelry, a thin gold bracelet and a string of pearls, she went down to the living room, which she found already crowded by those who clearly felt entitled and were enjoying champagne and hors d'oeuvres served by a small silent army of waiters in smart white jackets.

Studying them, Kelsie found herself wondering what sort of people would so ignore any standard of decency as to voluntarily come near Soundview with the palatial mansion contaminated beyond redemption by Paulstein. The thought of the lives he had broken there made her shudder no less than the appalling affrontery to any good taste that was its occupation by his wife.

There was no way of knowing which of all the graying and balding older men was Bellistree. So, certain that Melissa would point her out to the Saugatuck president, she stood at the fringe of the swirl of guests and waited, observing as she did that while most of the graying older men were accompanied by women more or less their own age, a small number were being enlivened by women far younger—a few seemed still in their twenties, one even younger, and clearly there just for that purpose. They were attractive, beautifully mannered, and well-dressed and groomed, perhaps a little too much so. Something about them rang an "expensive escort girls" bell in Kelsie.

She'd hardly accepted a tulip of champagne from one of a half-dozen waiters bearing it on a silver tray when she found herself suddenly confronted by a big fleshy overweight balding man with the face of a frog, looking down at her with a frown, and who had appeared so uncomfortably close to her that she could smell his shaving lotion.

"You are Kelsie Gordon?"

"I am," Kelsie replied, "and I take it you are Mr. Anthony Bellistree."

Bellistree's acknowledgment was simply to stare at her a moment with pale, slightly bulging watery eyes and then say, "I have arranged a job for you in our research department at Saugatuck Investments. You will be teamed with another of our researchers, a Mr. Randal Sherman. Your cubicle will be the one next to his. He's been told, and he will give all necessary instructions on all matters pertaining to the job. Office hours are from nine to five for employees. You begin tomorrow."

"I shall want a full tour of the building before I start," Kelsie said, barely managing to hide a smile and certain that Melissa had told him why she was there. And with no reason to conceal why that was, she went on to say, "And may I remind you, sir, that I will be at Saugatuck Investments courtesy of the U.S. government. Although I shall maintain strictest employer-employee protocol, I will need unlimited access to files, whether paper or electronic."

Bellistree's response was again to stare at her wordlessly, his lifeless eyes betraying no emotion, and then without a word abruptly turn his back on her and walk off.

That's right, shrink away, Kelsie thought. That

he did so told her he was a man who resented being spoken to by a woman as an equal.

More importantly, it told her that she had her work cut out for her. She was certain that, if for no reason other than principle and plain chauvinism, he was going to stonewall any attempt by her to learn by whom and to where the massive sums of money she'd traced to Saugatuck Investments were going. But while she was hardly undercover where he was concerned, she doubted if the same was true with anyone else at the company. Bellistree, she was sure, was a man constantly suspecting others, no matter what. He was not one to tolerate any of his employees knowing about any aspect of his business except for the limited area they were assigned to.

Kelsie's last sight of him was his joining another man of obvious stature in the world of wealth who appeared amusing to two very on-the-make and far younger women, who didn't appear to be American and whose makeup, low-cut dresses, and stiletto heels suggested only one motive. It made Kelsie wonder. Was Melissa, with lingering connections to young women desperate to leave Belarus and elsewhere, even if illegally, continuing to assist her husband's predilections where other men were concerned? She helped herself to a handful of hors d'oeuvres and another tulip of champagne, then fled back to her room.

Ignoring the faint sounds of the dinner below, she remembered that she'd promised

Gareth she'd call him with a report on her first day there. She dialed his cell and was relieved when he answered, and that he sounded sober and drug-free, and wanted at once to know where she was.

"In a rat's nest in Connecticut. Tell you all about it later. I'll be back before you know it. Will I find you sane and sober?"

"You will. Guaranteed."

"Scout's honor?"

He laughed. "From Cub to Eagle."

Loading him with warnings and instructions, she thought, *Jesus, I really* am *getting to be a bloody mom,* but when they'd both hung up, she felt a wave of relief. She could always tell from his voice if Gareth was on the straight and level. Angel's death was what had set him off. When he was in high school, somebody had got to him, first with pot, then cocaine, and then harder stuff. If she could ever find the person, she'd kick their head in. Meanwhile she could only say thank God he was off the stuff at present, and to desperately hope that the longer he was, the lesser the chance that he ever would get back on it.

Not ready for bed, she was wondering what she would do for dinner, and feeling a little at odds and ends, when Agnes, the maid, suddenly appeared with a tray.

"I thought you would like to dine, madam, since there didn't seem any place set for you below."

Kelsie was effusive with thanks, and even

more so when Agnes produced a bottle of wine and quickly uncorked it. "If there is anything else, madam, just ring for me. I'll keep an ear open, and if I'm in the dining room, Cook will tell me."

She left, and Kelsie, realizing how hungry she'd become, went to work on the tray, and poured out the wine. She had barely finished when there was a knock on her door. *Has to be Agnes again,* she thought, and she rose and went to open it. But it wasn't Agnes. It was Grisham.

Sixteen

There was a moment's dead silence before Grisham said, "Miss Gordon, I hope I am not disturbing you, but I wonder if you could spare a minute?"

In spite of her formality, she looked unaccustomedly nervous, and Kelsie, completely surprised, said, "Sure." And gestured at a chair.

Grisham came in, closing the door behind her, but didn't sit. Maintaining her formality, she said, "I need to speak to you about what you were doing downstairs before dinner."

"I was speaking to Mr. Bellistree. What else?"

"I was referring to your photographing dinner place cards. Was there some reason for it?"

"Goodness, Miss Grisham. How did you come to know that?"

"William reported it to me."

"The butler. Ah, I see. Is there any reason I shouldn't have?"

"It's a private dinner, Miss Gordon."

"And private people don't like where they are dining revealed?"

"Miss Gordon, there's something you ought to know. There's an audio line from the terrace to my office. When you came in this morning to introduce yourself to Mrs. Paulstein, she had opened it. She usually does. She likes to avoid repeating to me various orders to servants."

Ah, so that was it, Kelsie thought. Ten to one Grisham was worried for her job. If her photographing got to Melissa, she might get the sack no matter how valuable she was. A further thought flickered quickly. Grisham might someday prove to be a valuable ally.

She said, "So you heard me announce that I work for the United States Treasury and need Mrs. Paulstein to help place me in a job at Saugatuck Investments."

"Exactly."

"Miss Grisham, given your question as to why I was photographing place cards, perhaps you'd like to answer a question of mine. Why did four cards have no names on them?"

"They were last minute guests, Miss Gordon."

"And each one barely twenty, and probably foreign."

"Their age or where they come from is none of my business. Nor I should think of the Treasury Department."

"Possibly that's right. But I'm sure you know why, more likely than not, they're here. So let's put a few other simpler cards on the table. My interest in the blank cards has nothing to do with them but rather with the men they've been seated next to. Your worry is that an issue might be made of it and that you might find yourself involved. So to keep us both happy and unworried, may I suggest we both regard everything just said here as completely confidential, that our meeting never happened, and that I never photographed anything."

When Grisham suddenly wore an expression of one whose efforts have run into a wall, Kelsie added, "Oh, come on, Miss Grisham. Sit down and have what's left of the wine. I'm sure you could use it. You personally have absolutely nothing to do with why I am on my way to Saugatuck Investments, and I assure you that you are not being investigated."

Grisham's expression changed to one of relief, and she sank into the proffered chair. Kelsie immediately used every social skill she had learned in the various embassies of European capitals while on her pursuit of the laundered money. She made a point of being friendly and praised Grisham at length for the job she was doing, which she said, "must be appallingly difficult, given the mercurial character of your employer." And to make sure, she bombarded her with questions about it.

When Grisham departed over an hour later, it was to leave behind her the distinct impression that she couldn't stand Melissa Paulstein much longer. "I come from people with quite different standards," she'd said, and was only waiting, she'd added, for another job to turn up before leaving.

Kelsie knew then she had no further worries from her, and had even possibly won an ally.

That proved correct almost immediately. Grisham was halfway out the door when she stopped and turned, looking back.

"I seem to have forgotten my manners," she said. "Thank you for the wine, Miss Gordon. And your frankness. I think you might want to avoid the front stairs and Mrs. Paulstein while you are here. There's a back stair that's more convenient that guests often use. Its door is right across the hall from your room and it leads to a corridor that goes directly onto the parking area. The door there has a keypad, and the number is 323." She smiled. "Good luck with your investigation," and with that, she was gone.

There was still a drop of wine left. When Kelsie finished it off, the effect of the long day finally got the better of her.

"Tomorrow, Gordon," she said aloud, "you start work, so get some sleep." She got into bed and turned off the light, wondering as she did what Randal Sherman would be like and what she would uncover at Saugatuck Investments. The sooner she nailed everything she was up there for, the better, and the sooner she'd be back home in Washington.

Seventeen

Joshua Marshall stared blankly at nothing while fiddling uselessly with the pencil he'd plucked from the surface of his desk, cluttered by a Southern Poverty Law Center calendar and all the odd papers and memoranda he was working on. He twirled the pencil between thumb and forefinger back and forth without even being aware of doing so. It was a typical gesture of his when trying to think out a problem or come to an understanding about something. This time, the problem, as he thought of it, was FinCen's undercover agent in Connecticut.

Making a habit of always delving into people's backgrounds, he'd done so with her, first from idle curiosity, then intensively when he found a gap that vaguely disturbed him. In reading the extensive FBI background check on her that he and others at FinCen always underwent, he'd noted everything in her past, school and college records, the jobs she'd held before FinCen, but had seen no mention of her parents, except the name Gordon, Roger and Barbara.

Who were they, then? What was their niche in life, their professions or jobs if both worked? It disturbed him that the FBI had left such a blank in her past. Could it possibly and disturbingly be that all references to them had been deleted? Or that someone had abruptly ordered, "Go no farther." And, if so, who?

Joshua had a strength that was the driving force behind his rapid rise through the SPLC, the FBI, and then FinCen. That strength was his curiosity. From his earliest years on a share-cropper cotton farm in Alabama, he had wanted to know everything about everything, from "Did earthworms become two living worms if you cut one in half?" to "Did moths see in the dark or just flutter about blindly?" and later, when in his teens, to "Was a white president a constitutional requirement?"

Revealing the gap in Agent Gordon's past wasn't really necessary to keeping track of what she was currently doing, but any gap, no matter how insignificant, could spell trouble. But where to start?

"That's all very well, Joshua, but you're not just looking into her for security reasons." That came from his wife, Elaine, over breakfast coffee when he had explained his worry. She worked for a senator but hadn't dressed yet and was still in the pajamas he'd bought her for Christmas.

"I'm not?"

"No. I mean, I'm married to a wonderful guy who's always worried about the safety of stray dogs and cats, remember?"

"What do you mean? She's as tough as nails, a real hard-boiled case."

"Is she really?" His wife laughed. "I don't think so. Not from all you've told me."

And Joshua realized that deep down he really didn't think so either. Something at some time had sneaked out from behind the ice.

"Is she married?"

"No."

"Lesbian?"

"Don't believe so."

"Boyfriend?"

"Not that we know of."

"Then, why not? From what you've told me she's not unattractive."

"True."

"And in her thirties? She's got to be lonely, and hiding that even from herself."

"Possibly."

"Not possibly, and I know you. You've seen a vulnerable someone who needs protecting."

"More likely protecting FinCen," he'd laughed, and finished breakfast, fondly kissed Elaine, and headed off for his office. And all the way there, he kept thinking. *Had he?* Behind all the anger and cold disdain, was there indeed something else? Had he really sensed in her someone who needed help? She was an undercover agent tested in the Mafia world of Brooklyn, New York, when working for the DA, and untouchable, at least on the record. Look how she'd weathered the guy getting his brains blown out right in front of her. Yes, all of that. But. And he was still churning it over and over when it came to lunchtime.

Eighteen

Charles Wheeler had no such worries about Kelsie. At the end of the day and seated comfortably in a deep leather lounge chair in the bar of the exclusive Ivy League club off Connecticut Avenue, he saw her as a pawn in a game far larger than himself or anyone at Fin-Cen. It was a game that, if it didn't self-destruct, could possibly bring him down with it, and the irony of this and his role in it sometimes struck him, as it did tonight when a scotch and soda was brought to him on a tray by an obsequious uniformed waiter.

But after passing a moment or two greeting the occasional friends, all seemingly tied together through prep school, Harvard, Yale, or Princeton, Wheeler stopped any ironic laughter within himself and began to gratefully shred his working day and to feel free of the commonness he saw in all of it. He was back in a haven of WASP existence that he felt to be his heritage and which had been his life until he had been tossed to the mercy of the working world by the failure of his bankrupt father to leave him a dependable trust income when he died.

Presently, he pulled out his cell and punched in a number. His call was answered almost at once.

"Bellistree."

"Charles Wheeler, Tony. Checking to see how your new employee is working out."

"The Gordon girl? She's going nowhere. I've paired her with a hopeless nerd with orders to tie her hands and feet."

"Doing what?"

"Research."

"Good. Keep her out of investments."

"Wouldn't hurt if she went there. We don't file anything on paper. Whatever would be of concern, you and your special account is encrypted in my computer. Would take a master hacker to fish it out and make anything of it."

"Keep it that way."

Charles ended the call abruptly. He didn't have to show even a semblance of politeness with Bellistree. He had him in his pocket as successfully as he did Melissa Paulstein. Bellistree had escaped a fraud charge years ago, common knowledge said, thanks to unknown political pressure. All thought that some federal judge had known where his future would lie if he didn't dismiss the case as invalid. Wheeler had felt a certain smug satisfaction that in researching Bellistree afterward, when he'd assumed the helm of Saugatuck Investments, along with his close association with the vice president, he'd come across evidence of payoffs both to the state's prosecuting attorney and to the judge as well. Revelation of it wouldn't let Bellistree escape any longer regardless of his cronyism with his client VP.

It was only after he had hailed a passing bar waiter, and ordered another scotch, and settled deep in the lounge chair that Charles suddenly remembered that he hadn't received his usual daily report from Agent Gordon. That struck him as odd. Perhaps she was unable to for some reason. If he hadn't heard from her by tomorrow, he'd text her to demand to know why not.

He was glad to have heard from Bellistree that he had her successfully tied up, and began to laugh inwardly again at the irony of the whole situation.

Nineteen

In her two weeks working at Saugatuck Investments, Kelsie avoided Melissa like the plague. The maid, Agnes, brought her meals on a tray if she didn't eat at a diner in town, and morning and night she crept in and out of the mansion by the back stair Grisham had told her about. It led first to a long carpeted corridor, its walls lined with expensive prints of nineteenth-century racing yachts, then at its end to a door onto the parking area. Agnes, the maid, had added color to its convenience by telling her tales of the celebrities who used it. "You wouldn't believe the sneaking in and out when cheating on their regulars," the young maid had said.

At work she had to face that she'd achieved very little. It had taken days of make-believe to bond even slightly with an awkwardly shy and distant Randal Sherman. He had at first been completely stand-offish, seeming to regard her as an unwanted intrusion into his particular fiefdom of research and a threat to his job.

Equally difficult was getting the hang of the

place and in satisfying the curiosity of the other researcher in the division that rarely saw any newcomer. Everyone wanted to know about her past job and experience, where she had worked and lived before Saugatuck Investments. The questions were endless, but Kelsie was well prepared for that with a faked resume she'd concocted, which seemed to satisfy them all, and it wasn't long before she ceased to be a novelty.

Then, when she was no longer seen as that, there were long hours, many after work, or very early before work began, spent in surreptitious investigation of files that were totally unconnected with the research department, and the research that she was supposed to be doing as her cover, where everyone save for Bellistree was concerned. She had tracked the money coming from the Mexican company to Saugatuck Investments and knew it was there, but where? And if and when she found out to whom it was finally being dispersed, would it be in time before it maddingly disappeared, not all at once, she was certain, but in sum by sum without any indication of where it was going.

Meanwhile, and though she was certain the various white nationalist hate groups it was slated for were undoubtedly hiding behind corporate identities, she failed to turn up which ones. After checking the company's Management Division and its Corporate Assets Division, and settling on its Investment Division, she could still find no companies receiving money that were not long-standing and impeccable clients whose revenues rarely showed any unexplained increase.

And yet someone was undoubtedly already getting some of it, and the someone had to be one or more hate groups, unless she was all wrong on the whole laundering business, as well as the whistle-blower, Mohammed Adi, and she firmly believed he hadn't been, nor she. With acute discomfort, she could only come to the conclusion that she was being cleverly stonewalled.

Her search of investment and learning and getting to understand its workings took time and brought her to realize that if she were to learn anything, she desperately needed an ally, and that would have to be Randal. He had proven himself more than ordinarily bright, and for reasons that evaded her because he was stuck in a cubicle, he seemed to have an extraordinary knowledge of virtually every department and everyone who worked in the place. A serious bond of some sort with him might prove useful.

She began to study him so as to figure the best way first to approach, then to enlist. He had consistently been formality itself, first distant, then polite, then helpful, but always quite formal and never friendly. She'd been rather the same way herself, and decided to change tactics. She started by bringing a small plant for him to put on his desk one morning, for which she received surprised and stammered thanks that gave her a chance for a headlong assault.

She put on a warmest smile and said, "Thought to brighten your day a little. You're so burdened with me." And then, breaking into yet more stammered protests, "Randal, there are a lot of things about my job I can't really ask you here in the office. Can't we have lunch sometime?"

"Lunch?"

"Yes. Don't look so surprised. We're hardly strangers."

"Well, er—If you want, I—I can try to find a corner in the cafeteria."

"I didn't mean the cafeteria. I meant someplace else where we can't be heard. At the diner in town, for example."

It was like pulling teeth. He seemed truly worried that leaving the building and perhaps overstaying the hour allowed for lunch could cost him his job. To say nothing of lunching alone with a young woman away from the job.

"Not if you're with me."

"But you don't know Bellistree."

"I have leverage where Bellistree is concerned."

"Leverage?"

"Leverage."

She ignored his open-mouthed surprise, and the next day, a few minutes before it was official office lunchtime, with virtually all the employees preparing to leave their desks or cubicles for the cafeteria, she insisted they slip away. Again ignoring his protests, she took advantage of him not wanting to be seen or overheard by others in the research department, and hustled him out of the building to her car before he could effectively say no. And then, after a dead silent drive to the diner, during which he sat frozen with what she could only conclude was embarrassed anxiety, she had almost to drag him inside and to a booth.

One lunch led to two, a few days later, and during the course of the second one, and even though Randal constantly looked at his watch, he began to loosen up a little. At one point, he even became talkative, and goaded by Kelsie, became guardedly critical of Saugatuck Investments.

"How—how do you like being here?" he said.

"Frankly, I'd rather be elsewhere. How about you?"

"It's a job."

"That's all? What would you really like to be doing?"

"Do you know France?"

"Yes."

"You can take a barge down their canals from Belgium all the way to the Atlantic."

"You'd like to do that?"

"I'd like to own one of those barges. Live on it."

It was Kelsie's turn to stare open-mouthed. The French barge canals were an idyllic escape from reality, hundreds of miles of sleepy drifting through the French countryside, far from cities, even large towns, and no tourists, only the old France that used to be before the automobile.

Listening to Randal describe them, she realized she was sharing the vision of a desperately lonely man who felt unfulfilled, and worse, unwanted, one who found solace in his job by escape into a romantic fantasy of forbidden or unaffordable adventurism, and she began to see him in quite a different way than she saw him at work. It made her wonder how he could stand being in such a dreary place as an investment company, and quite to her surprise, she found, also, that she quite liked him. Behind his rather nerdy exterior and awkward shyness there was a completely different person.

The interludes were brief. Each time on the way back to work, Randal became silent and formal again. Once there and back in their cubicles with his again seeming reluctance to answer her questions on research, it was as though they had never been to lunch at all. Kelsie realized she was going to have to work much harder to get him as a truly conspiratorial ally. Talking about his escapist dreams might be the way to do it, and she determined to take him to lunch again, better still to dinner, as soon as she could unbend him again.

Twenty

Waking, it took a moment or two for Gareth to realize that the house was dead quiet. Kelsie had to be at work. Why didn't he hear her in the kitchen as usual. And then he remembered—she'd d gone off on the job to Connecticut someplace. He wished she'd tell him what she did on all these trips. She never had. It was just like that when he was much younger and she was chasing about in Brooklyn. It was as though there were two Kelsies: his sister at home looking after him by cooking meals and all that, but nagging him about drugs like she was a mother, and a Kelsie who disappeared from time to time and about whom he knew nothing.

He checked his bedside digital clock. The blurred red numbers said nine something. Nine thirty? Jesus. He'd overslept. Rising, he realized why. His head was logy from a hangover, and he began to remember the night before. Drugs? No. Not drugs. He hadn't done any, not even cocaine. He'd made an effort and stayed off them, even when everyone else was doing them, including his latest female target. He'd tell the therapist and especially Kelsie so he could get a medal pinned on him instead of a cascade of berating fury. No, this time it was good old-fashioned drink. Endless glasses of some damn thing with rum in it. He cursed. No more rum. Not ever.

He'd managed a shower and had gotten himself downstairs for coffee when he heard a knock on the front door. Thinking *What the hell?* he went, unlocked and opened it, and found himself looking at a big powerful well-dressed dark-skinned guy.

"Yes?"

"George Duval. ICE. We've had a report you had illegals using you as a refuge."

"Illegals?"

"Yes."

"Not here. You've got the wrong house."

"I'll have to check. Mind if I come in?" Joshua flashed his official ID, but only long enough for Gareth to see the U.S. seal on one corner.

"Yeah, I guess. Help yourself. But hurry it up. I have a class at eleven."

"School?"

"American University."

"Really? That's my alma mater." Joshua pushed past Gareth, and after a brief glance in the kitchen, made his way into the living room and saw the scattered lacrosse equipment.

"You're lacrosse?"

"Varsity."

"That's great. I did football." Then, "Nice place. Do you share?"

"My sister and I. We own it."

"Really. What does she do?"

"Who the hell knows? Works at something for the government. Treasury, I think, but she won't ever talk about it. She spent months in Europe this year. Sent me postcards and called a lot and all that, but you tell me what she was doing." He laughed, looked at his watch and then said, "Look, what's this illegals business? There's just me and my sister here."

Boy wants me out, Joshua thought. He said, "I can see that. Don't know where the report came from. We get that sort of crank call all the time, and we're obliged to check it out. Where's your sister?"

"Working."

Joshua's eye fell on the framed photograph of Angel. "Who's this?"

"That's our mother."

It caught Joshua completely off guard. "Your mother?" He glanced again at the photo as though he'd missed something, and then at Gareth. There was no sign Gareth had been facetious.

Gareth saw his confusion and smiled. "Yeah, I know. That came out of me automatically. She wasn't our real mother. Just our guardian, but she was mother to us for as long as I can remember. She was a nurse."

"Oh? And your real mother?"

"Hardly knew her. I was in grade school

when she died. Cancer."

"Sorry to hear that." Joshua nodded at the photo. "So, she was sort of your semi-mom. For how long?"

"Years. Mom left her the house, and then she left it to us."

"Interesting. What was her name?"

"Angel."

"Angel? Angel what?"

"Savannah. She always said she got it from her great-grandfather who was landed there as a slave whenever. A good while before the Civil War, I guess."

Joshua glanced again at the framed photograph. She was beautiful, he thought. The kids had been lucky. There was warmth and intelligence and love written all over her. How had she ever ended up as guardian to two white kids? Joshua knew when he'd hit real evidence of some kind, and decided before he left to have one last try for more.

"What happened to your father?"

A shadow flickered across Gareth's face. Joshua saw it. Gareth said, "Never knew him either. Died before I was born."

"Oh? When?"

"Don't know."

That's hard, Joshua thought. Not to know who your father was. It could explain something about his sister, though, some of her toughness. Clearly she was now the "man" in the family with all the responsibilities that entailed. Did this boy know the extent of what she did to make a living? Somehow, he doubted that he did.

"Look—I'll be late for class."

"Sure. Sorry for the intrusion. I'll give you an all clear on illegals. And good luck at lacrosse."

"Thanks."

Back outside, Joshua wondered again. How had two white kids end up with a black foster mother? Finding that out, he thought, might well be the key to the gap in Kelsie Gordon's past that he sought to fill.

Twenty-One

Leaving her cubicle at close to quitting time, Kelsie found her way out of the office unexpectedly blocked by Randal. Red in the face, he stammered a suggestion that she dine with him if she didn't have anything more important to do. He knew, he said, a neat restaurant with Mexican food.

"Mostly working class Latinos, all speaking Spanish, and I don't," he said apologetically, "but the food is great. And they've got some guy there every night who plays a mean guitar."

It caught Kelsie completely off guard. It had been several days since she'd taken Randal to the diner for lunch, and she had wondered how to ask him to dinner. He'd been a little more open and helpful with work than before, but she never suspected such forwardness from him. If she was surprised by it, she was no less surprised by her own unhesitant acceptance of his invitation. Without even thinking or preparing any sort of strategy, she'd heard herself say, "Sure, why not? Sounds fun."

Instinctively wary, however, as on any first date, she insisted first on going Dutch, then on driving there in her own car while he drove in his, readily finding a reason for not wanting to come back to collect hers after dinner.

The Mexican dinner led to a Chinese one two days later, with Randal becoming more and more relaxed and insisting they didn't talk business. Bit by bit, while revealing little of her own life, past or present, she got him to talk about himself: where he'd worked before, and his college years, where he'd lived, his favorite reading in all the classics, which turned out to be the French writer and activist Émile Zola, who had always been her favorite too. And finally, his parents: did his father still work, did his mother still play in the philharmonic? Were they still part of his life? They were, and Randal was fond of them both.

It was on a third and pleasantly friendly meal in the Rive Bistro, a lovely very French place on the Saugatuck River close to the sound, with Randal coming almost completely out of his shell and with herself comfortably, even seriously enjoying him, that he asked her what she did in her spare time. When she waffled, realizing that she rarely if ever had any outside work interests or time for anything other than her brother, he said suddenly, "I'd love to trust you with something."

"What? What is it?"

"It very secret."

"Secret? Goodness," she laughed. "Is it something kinky, or something you shouldn't be doing?"

Randal looked around to make sure nobody could hear, and lowered his voice almost to a whisper.

"You won't tell anybody?"

"Not if you ask me not to."

"Promise?"

"Of course."

"It's something I shouldn't be doing," he said, "here at work."

"What?"

"I hack."

"You do *what?*"

"I hack. I see what's what with all the uptight bunch we work with. Look into all their emails and stuff."

It was the very last thing Kelsie ever would have thought of, and when she at first simply gaped wordlessly, he went on to say, "I often go back to the office and spend my evenings at it. I've got really good."

It was so completely unlikely and unsuspected that something about it made Kelsie burst into laughter, and for a moment she couldn't stop, until aware that Randal was looking anxious, even worried that he ever should have trusted her. And yet it fitted with his knowing so much about all the different people in Saugatuck Investments' many departments when locked all day, every day, in his cubicle. Everything he knew and said about them had come from his ability to widely spy on everyone.

That brought her to a sudden stop. A deathly silence fell between them, broken only by the clatter of silver and the muted conversation of other diners. The restaurant around her, the candlelit table at which she sat with Randal, even Randal himself, all momentarily disappeared, along with the rare intimacy of a pleasant evening, before a cold realization of who she was and who he was. She was investigating high state crimes, he was part of the organization she was investigating. Or was he?

Paranoia seized, brought on by her professional experience and especially by the mess she'd found herself in when having coffee with Mohammed Adi.

Who was Randal? Why was it he didn't fit with any of the other employees? Was he a plant just the same as she was? But a Russian one? Or possibly from the EU, which could explain his love of France. Was all the shyness and stammering and general embarrassment just a cover for similar ruthlessness? Had she, for all her usual caution, fallen into a trap? It flitted through her mind that she had been wise to always go to dinner with him in separate cars. It ruled out that she might be found a bound and gagged murdered body floating down the Saugatuck River.

But then, at the same time, there was the remembered casual remark from one of the few researchers more or less friendly. "Haven't you noticed? Everyone else has. The whole department. The nerd's positively got a crush on you."

She stared at Randal, at his boyish face and worried eyes, his charmingly attractive unruly hair. And when he simply stared back, and with the most innocently trusting expression, the paranoia ebbed away. She realized how much she had come to care for him, and with a flood of emotion, intimacy returned and told her that he had to be real, that this wasn't some sort of clever Russian or right-wing extremist about to expose her real role at Saugatuck. She shook her head and placed a hand on one of his. "Oh, Randal, you are one in a million."

"You don't hate me?"

"No. Don't be silly. Actually, it sounds like fun, and I'm sure it's harmless enough. As long as you never use any of the dirt you must collect."

"Never," Randal said.

She said, "Just who do you hack? I mean, only people in research, or what?"

"Sky's the limit."

"Bellistree?"

"Oh, that fat hog." Randal laughed. "Of course. He's most entertaining of all. He's into a lot of those neo-Nazi groups. Took a while to figure out his password, but I finally nailed it. It's Nero. Kind of fits, huh?"

It took Kelsie's breath away. Once again, she was taken by surprise. The word everyone in intelligence wanted explained. She managed to cover. "Nero, the Roman emperor?"

"The same. But it's apparently not just his password. I pick up the odd thing in some of Bellistree's emails that Nero is also some person, and that not only is he using Nero as a password, but that a lot of the supremacist groups are too."

Kelsie could hardly believe what she was hearing. She studied him. It was all so totally unexpected, so incredible. Eight hours ago, she'd had nothing. Now and out of nowhere, a possible crack, not only in Bellistree's stonewalling but an insight into a lot more.

"I'm going back tonight. Care to join me?"

"Suppose someone returns. Late work, or they forgot something."

"We're working overtime, and who's to know what you've got going on a computer?"

Kelsie swallowed a slight sense of guilt at the realization that she would be blatantly using Randal when he thought her friendly and safe, and that they were only having fun. But wasn't that what she was there for?

Memories of her DA work chasing down Mafia dons, her work with the FBI on counterterrorism, and now all the work she'd so far done with FinCen came into her head.

She said. "When do we start?"

Twenty-Two

Melissa lay luxuriating in the deep warming comfort of her bath, and after taking a sip of the margarita, put it back on the tray that traversed the tub just above the scented foam made by bath salts. She'd gone to New York to spend a day shopping, and she let sensuous sensations course up through her body.

For some time before the discovery of her husband's lurid activities that led to his arrest, she had become aware of them, and aware of how he went about his procuring. One of several ways was through an employment agency in New York specializing in escort girls, and Paulstein had taken the trouble to cultivate the woman who owned it, who, for the money involved, overcame any suspicions she had as to why he might want such help. The knowledge enabled Melissa to find young dates for those seemingly respectable businessmen whom Bellistree told her were white nationalists and clients of Saugatuck Investments. Invitations to them for her parties with the added attraction of young women free to make their own arrangements for anything else afterward was a smart way, he said, to keep tabs on their business activities, important due to the financial relationships they had with the investment firm.

When the landline phone rang from where it was conveniently hung on the mirrored wall close to her head, she frowned, and for a moment rejected answering it. Calls on it were almost invariably from Wheeler or Bellistree. She didn't feel like talking to either. She lifted the receiver with a wet hand. "Yes?"

"Charles."

"And?"

"What's happening with your guest?"

"Who?"

"You know who. The Gordon woman."

"I wouldn't know. I never see her. Bellistree took her on."

"I may dump her."

"Oh?"

"I'm not getting her reports as ordered, so I'll be coming up in a few days. Bellistree should know, and I'll want to talk with him. Have him there."

"Exactly when?"

"You'll hear from me."

A click and the line went dead. Melissa cursed and put the receiver back. She took a long hard sip of the margarita to help erase his call, then sank deeper in the bath and let her mind wander back to the evening and day and evening again she'd spent with Boris Sokolov, and the agreement they had. Her part was to keep him informed on anything she picked up about the Wheeler woman, as she called the guest she was stuck with boarding and for whom she'd been required to find a job.

Something about Wheeler's call nagged. She wasn't quite sure what, and debated a moment before making up her mind, and passing on her landline, which Wheeler had bugged, she was sure, she took up her cell instead, pressing a button that protected the call from scrutiny before punching in the number.

It rang, and a deep voice answered. "Melissa?"

"Yes."

"Are we secure?"

"I've had my phone fixed so we can be." Then, "Our deal. My part. There's something going on with either Wheeler or his agent. He's been pulled, and she's started reporting to someone else in Washington. I think someone more important. I thought it was something you would want to know."

"Thank you. I'll take it from there."

"When do we meet again?"

"I have to visit the VP at his fishing lodge in Maine. Maybe when I get back."

Was that an excuse not to? Melissa didn't think so. His tone had said he was interested. But she played it safe. Boris Sokolov was not a man to be pushed. She said matter-of-factly, "See you then, maybe. Enjoy fishing." She ended the call and sank back down deep in the soothingly warm scented water.

At the same time, Bellistree too leaned back, but in his deeply comfortable office chair and with a definite feeling of satisfaction, while carefully folding the eyes-only handwritten report he'd received only moments before from Pat Simmons in the investment department, in an envelope she'd carefully sealed and hand-delivered.

Presently, he rose and took it across his carpeted office to the shredder that sat next to his copier and watched it disappear, to come out a moment later in tiny unreadable strips, which he dumped in a scrap basket.

Back at his desk, he picked up his office phone.

"Pat Simmons."

"Good job, Pat."

"Thanks, Tony."

"Did you spread it thin?"

"Six people worked on it, each with a tiny section. They haven't a clue."

"Your computer? You kept it in code before printing it?"

"Yes, sir."

Bellistree mentally matched an image to the voice at the other end of the line. Pat Simmons saw white nationalism the same way he did, as the only way to save America from weak-sister liberals, and from the Blacks and Latinos who supported them. She secretly belonged to one of the more virulent neo-Nazi racist groups that he occasionally visited himself and which regularly received a sizeable cash bonus from him for carefully disseminating very large sums of money to half a dozen smaller groups hiding behind respectable corporate names and respectable businesses. She also provided him with sexual relief in the office whenever he felt the need for it. She was an overweight brassy-looking overly dyed blonde in her late fifties, with large breasts and a whisky tenor voice, but was a master, he'd discovered, at giving head. To further ensure her silence about money disbursements as well, he'd secretly videotaped every one of their unions.

"You might drop by my office sometime late this afternoon, Pat. The usual."

"Yes, sir. Will do."

Bellistree put the phone back down.

Twenty-Three

Marie Suarez wasn't altogether sure in the reports she received from Kelsie Gordon about the Randal Sherman person. It wouldn't be the first time she'd seen an agent completely taken in by an adversary they had overly trusted. In the centuries-long history of espionage, there had been countless cases of such, and she herself had seen equally blameless people who, after exemplary clearance, had astonished veteran investigators by turning out to be the worst sort of fraudsters and double-dealers.

Gordon had proved as usual to be first class with intelligence and nerves of steel. It was nearly impossible to doubt the trustworthiness of either her or her reports. But her judgment of this Sherman person she was now computer hacking with would have to remain suspect until proven otherwise. No matter her constant assurances that her fellow researcher was okay; no matter too that looking into his past at her request, the FBI had discovered only an exemplary background and nothing even remotely suspicious, no matter that he had come up with the specific person in the investment department reporting to Bellistree, and the amounts she was disbursing from an unregistered ancillary organization known as the South West Trust.

And no matter, finally, that Bellistree, in turn, was using in his emails a password, Nero, which apparently was also used by multiple different nationalist groups and which referred to some unknown person. It was the kind of information that while seemingly bona fide could possibly turn up false, and if it did, in her experience it could destroy a case along with the people who had spent years building it.

She had to take that risk, however, and for the moment there was another thought that had begun to bother her constantly. With memory of the murder of Mohammed Adi still fresh, had she possibly placed Gordon in similar mortal danger? She and Joshua Marshall had already talked about the white-collar world of finance in Europe, and how Saugatuck Investments in relatively law-abiding Connecticut had little if anything in common with the murderous thugs harbored in the alarmingly increasing number of white nationalist organizations. Neo-Nazis didn't mess around. They simply eliminated, often with almost unheard of sadism and brutality. The Saudi whistle-blower in a way had been lucky. He'd been finished off with a single shot. Women who were suspect, as Joshua had amply shown in the video, were kept alive and usually subjected to far worse.

She called in Joshua and told him how she felt.

"It all depends on how close she's getting," Joshua said. "Has she actually visited any of the organizations?"

"She hasn't reported that she has."

"Just the same."

"Just the same what? Are you thinking I should recall her, perhaps replace her with some tough bastard who if caught might be able to talk them into letting him join up without having to submit to gang rape to prove it, or maybe fight his way out?"

"Something like that. Yes."

"But, like who? Again, Joshua, our budget getting slashed limits us to almost no one who answers that description and who, at the same time, would be smart enough to take on a case at the point Gordon has reached." Anxiety over the state of her money-short department had begun to overcome Suarez's anxiety over Kelsie. She followed with, "Maybe we should give her a little longer, see how far she gets with hacking. Then I think a recall *would* be wise."

"You're the boss, and I think you're probably right." Joshua smiled, partially covering his reluctance to agree. "Maybe the metaphor isn't quite right. Gordon is an able young woman, but you don't pull a horse from a race a hundred yards from the finish line just because it just started to rain and made the track dangerous."

He paused, then added, "Getting any farther with your thoughts about that Russian, Sokolov? His connection to the VP?"

"I haven't. I felt I was allowing too much of my political feeling to interfere with my job. What do you think?"

"I wouldn't be so sacrosanct, Marie, if you'll forgive me for saying so. Everyone knows how blinded to reality the VP is by his religion. And particularly so when it comes to his relationships with dictators. Naivety can in its very innocence be as dangerous as treason. I'd pursue any thinking you might have on the subject. Like everyone else these days, we've run into a situation in which one might have to vote their intuitions and not by any rule book."

When Joshua had left her office, Marie said to herself, *He's right. I'll pursue it. And to hell with the consequences. You have to live up to your beliefs and follow them. If you don't, what's the point of it all?* The vice president was hardly known for agnostic unfettered intelligence, and who knows what stupidity he might inadvertently manage, or what damaging foreign policy he might commit the country to, given his blinding religious fervor.

It was a Tuesday. She scrawled on the Friday box of her desk calendar, "Possibly replace agent," and got back to other work.

Twenty-Four

Marie Suarez was unaware that at that very moment a potential threat to her agent, and a man she would have dearly loved to see put out of action by the FBI, had finished checking the tires and gas of his Honda 500 cc motorbike and was back in his room in a run-down motel on the far outskirts of Washington, DC, where he had holed up awaiting orders for his next job.

Although always well paid, Grigori Lebedev's personal standards had never risen above those of his roots in a Moscow slum, and his aspirations as to where and how he lived didn't rise higher than the room he currently occupied. It had long harbored a clinging smell of stale sweat and cigarettes, the bedspread was clearly in need of laundering, the curtains were plastic, the orange shag carpeting was noticeably stained. And the mostly naked woman he'd kept hanging about to have sex with when and if it pleased him was no better than any of it.

He ignored her when he came in. Flopping

down on the bed beside her and pushing away her hands, he flicked on the TV with its remote and ordered up the forensic crime channel that was his favorite, and then, when commercials came on, rose and went to pull aside the curtain that closed off shelves and a hanging space for clothes. There, from the protective covering of a leather jacket, he retrieved a shoulder holster that was home to his .45 automatic. Bringing it back to the bed, he resumed watching forensic experts doing their work while wiping the gun clean and reloading its clip from a box of cartridges stowed in a small bedside cabinet along with some gun oil, all the time ignoring the woman who rose and went to the bathroom.

Satisfied the gun was in perfect working order, he restored it to its holster and punched in a number on his cell. When it answered, he said only, his Russian accent heavy, "Grigori. Put Sokolov on." A moment while he listened, then he shouted angrily. "You heard me. Sokolov. And right now." Some angry words in Russian could be heard in reply before Sokolov came on the line, and Grigori, his own tone now quite different said, "Yes, sir. Lebedev. I'm returning a call you made to me yesterday. I only got the message this morning." He listened and then said, "Where do I work next? Oh?" And then, "Yes, sir. When?"

His question answered, he wordlessly put the receiver back on its stand, and when the woman retuned, said, "You—put some clothes on and get the fuck out of here. I'll be away for a couple of days. I'll maybe call you when I'm back."

As she silently obeyed, he decided he'd get rid of her like the last one—one shot and into the Potomac. Not a problem; she was illegal and had no papers, nobody would miss her. He thought, *I'll let Masha know I'll be up*, and resumed watching television.

Twenty-Five

Sometime while in the middle of speaking to Gareth, Joshua Marshall realized that with both Kelsie and her brother no longer children, the chance was slim that the obstetrician who delivered them, and who might have known the parents, would still be around. Checking first on Kelsie via her on-file background that she was born in Washington at the Sibley Memorial Hospital, Joshua found that to be so. But as he suspected, the doctor who had delivered her was long dead. He then ran into the same thing when trying to check on Kelsie's brother. And even worse, when he investigated the supposed parents of each, he discovered after lengthy research they were fictitious.

At a dead end, he knew that the only possible last chance way for him to go any farther might lie in investigating the children's once surrogate mother, Angel Savannah. It sounded simple enough, but he suspected that tracing Angel wasn't going to be easy either. And it wasn't.

Presuming she had died in Washington,

DC, the obvious route to her was the coroner's office. But the coroner of what district? There were several, so that seemed like a needle-in-a-haystack search. He could go laboriously through voting records and Social Security files but would need a court order for such official channels. Frustrated, he regretted that he had failed to ask Gareth a key question about her— had she been religious?

Taking a chance that she had been, he checked out various Washington churches, especially those in the relative neighborhood of the Capitol, and struck one, the Universal African Baptist, that had a predominately black congregation. He paid a call on the little church, whose shabby front was hardly recognizable as a religious refuge, and was glad he'd played the hunch when he was greeted at the vestry door by the deacon, a graying and affable man, who welcomed him without guile, and responded immediately as to whether he remembered a parishioner named Angel Savannah.

"Angel? Oh, but I do indeed," the old man said, his wrinkled face, which showed a long lifetime of experiencing all too often the sadness of others, wreathed immediately in an almost beatific smile. "The loveliest person I ever knew. She was an angel indeed."

To Joshua, getting him to talk about her role as Kelsie's and Gareth's surrogate mother was easy.

"If there were ten others in the whole United

States as devoted to her charges, as loving and as intelligent in their upbringing, I would see it as a miracle," the old man said.

When it came to going any farther than that, however, the deacon was quite openly reluctant to talk, and Joshua realized that he would have to go official.

He produced his ID and said, "Deacon, please don't be alarmed. There is nothing wrong. Kelsie Gordon is a highly esteemed colleague working for the Treasury Department, and we're not worried about any malfeasance on her part. We're only worried about trouble coming at her, not from her, and possibly only because of her past. We need to know more of that past in order to protect her."

The strategy, combined with assurance of complete confidentiality—"No word of this, Deacon, will ever go public"—worked. The deacon slowly began to unbend. The names of the mother and father on Gareth's birth certificate, he explained, were indeed fictitious. Both the children were illegitimate. Their mother, Andrea, had Gareth twelve years after Kelsie when Andrea had a brief affair with some unknown man at the start of her illness.

"Kelsie's father?" Joshua asked. "Who was he?"

There was a heavy silence, and when the deacon finally spoke, the revelation came to Joshua as a shock that for a moment rendered him speechless.

"Her father's name, sir, is Emanuel Arthur."

With difficulty, Joshua gathered himself and finally found words. He had opened a Pandora's box. "The vice president? Surely you can't mean it."

"Yes, sir. I'm afraid it's so. When Andrea died," the deacon went on, taking courage, "she willed the house to the kids and nominated Angel as their children's legal guardian until Kelsie reached her majority. At the same time, his high-priced lawyers buried any evidence of his paternity as well as his relationship with their mother.

"But he failed when he went after the house, and that brought out a lot of ugly racism in him. It wasn't just money; the man couldn't stand any house he owned handed over to someone same as you and me. And he found ways to make Angel's life hell because of it, poor woman. He threw the N-word at her every chance he got. He reviled her slave great-granddaddy as an animal. He had her hounded day and night for a spell, and threatened worse if she ever breathed a word of his paternity. And it wasn't enough that the poor woman woke in the morning scared half to death and went to bed at night the same way."

"And all the time, everything he was doing was silenced?"

"Yes, sir. Political strings and money in the right hands."

"How did Angel die? She was still only middle-aged, I take it."

"Yes, sir. And it wasn't anything like Andrea's

cancer. She died from something far worse. Angel was deliberately run down by a hit-and-run driver right in front of the oldest child, Kelsie. Killed instantly, and it wasn't pretty. Both kids still just students, Kelsie about to finish high school, Gareth still way back down the ladder. Rumor had it she was silenced to hide his paternity, but it never went anywhere. The police hushed it up, which we learned here in this church through an informer. And the pedestrian death of an unknown black woman didn't excite any interest in the press. Pedestrians are killed all the time in big cities."

"Hushed up? Hushed up how?"

"All the rumors said politics someplace, and Kelsie took them for proof that it was true. I tried to talk her out of it, but she kept clinging to it, and I guess still does. I was visiting her one day to offer comfort when he came by, wanting bad to get the house back so he could sell it, and she lit into him like a tiger, kicked and scratched him and swore if he ever showed his face near her and Gareth again she'd blow him away, and then marched him off with a handgun she'd got somehow."

Joshua felt a chill in his whole body.

"She never told Gareth who he was," the old man went on, "only that he was a landlord trying to steal their property for nothing because he wanted to tear the whole row down and put up a project. And Gareth being only just in elementary school took that in as gospel. They both go regularly to put flowers on Angel's grave, or visit me, so I know he's never found out about the vice president being his father. Kelsie, she keeps it entirely to herself."

After he'd left the deacon at the Universal African Baptist Church and was on his way back to his office, Joshua tried to add up what he'd heard. His first clear thought was never to repeat what he'd been told to Kelsie, and it wasn't until sometime after the day was over, and he was home and had a drink with his wife, and was watching the evening news on the TV, that he realized he was never going to tell anyone else either. If what he knew about Vice President Emanuel Arthur ever got out, his job at FinCen, like Kelsie's, as well as the future careers of both, would be over.

Twenty-Six

Kelsie stared at the calm slate-blue water from where she sat on a blue and white beach towel on the long crescent-shaped family beach where Westport met the sound. For a moment she was not speaking. Nothing seemed real since the murder of Mohammed Adi, not her meeting Melissa Paulstein and staying at the palatial Paulstein home, not finding herself working as a researcher at an often touted investment company, not, certainly, becoming friendly with the young man apparently responsible for introducing her to the firm and the work she was doing as a cover for why she was really there. And certainly not spending a Saturday with him on a beach.

What on earth was she doing here, having a picnic, a burning sun only half thwarted by the large beach umbrella he'd brought, and occasionally badgered by the endless seagulls fluttering close in searching a handout from the lunch and bottle of chilled white wine he'd also brought?

It was strictly a family beach; little children, in groups or singly, rushed around or built sand castles close to the water. A monumental Revolutionary War cannon placed on a platform graced the sand not far off; British troops had landed there before a long march inland in hopes of crushing the rebellion.

A slim young woman, not yet out of her teens, and identified by her red T-shirt emblazoned with a white cross and the words LIFE GUARD, sat silently on a small tower, gaped at in awe by small children while keeping watch over all of it.

Sanity, Kelsie thought. *The kind of life I ought to be leading and am not.*

Randal had suggested the beach after dinner the night before, and she'd agreed, although a little warily. Four nights of dining and several bottles of wine had revealed a shy but thoughtful young man with a personal charm that apparently had eluded everyone at Saugatuck Investments except her, for what reasons she couldn't fathom except that people tended to discriminate against any who they saw as different. His shyness and distancing himself from people hadn't helped.

But their dinners had also shown her quite another side of Randal. Even before their first night of hacking together was over, both giggling like schoolchildren at the personal lives of one person after another, and as Randal blithefully hacked through emails with an ease that astonished her, he revealed himself as a computer genius.

As she was steered through one hacking mystery after another in answer to her endless questions, she realized she'd discovered more than an invaluable teacher; she had indeed found herself an unwitting ally. As every minute passed with her sitting next to him, she had learned valuable elements of hacking, even on their first night, and their second night of hacking into coworkers now seemed a thing of some far distant past as more and more she had begun to see his hacking as a way for finally uncovering the disbursement from Saugatuck Investments of the laundered Russian money.

"Penny," she heard him say, and she slowly came to her senses.

"Nothing much. Just enjoying. I'm so glad we did this."

The "we" sounded to her a little like they were a couple, and she hoped he hadn't heard it that way. But her heart sank slightly when his next remark showed that he had—at least partway, or even with the hopeful though of perhaps one day getting there.

"I'm glad too," he said. And then, "Coming down to the beach has made me aware that I really know nothing about you, except superficially. I've told you a world of stuff about myself, but know nothing about you. Not really. I mean, where do you come from, what's your family is like, why you came to work at Saugatuck Investments? Do you have a boyfriend somewhere, or were you married once?"

It was a moment she'd dreaded. If she wanted to keep him as an ally, she had to find answers. She put on an air of gaiety she didn't feel. "I'm a wicked fallen woman with a black past."

He laughed with her, but then said, "Seriously."

She made him wait a moment, fishing desperately in her mind for answers that would satisfy. "No," she said finally. "I never married, although I once nearly did. And I don't have a boyfriend. At least not anymore. I ditched him two years ago."

She was rewarded by seeing him visibly brighten, while trusting at the same time that he wouldn't delve any deeper into either relationship, and relieved that she had at least told partial truths. There had been a chance at marriage while she'd worked in New York, but her concentration at work had blown it, and there's been a brief fling with a Belgian diplomat while abroad that had ended when she'd discovered he was married. When Randal asked about her parents, she decided to be frank, even if answering falsely. "Don't have any."

"What do you mean?"

"I was raised first in foster homes I can barely remember, then by a court-appointed guardian who died a while back."

"Gosh, that's sad."

"I guess. But I've managed okay."

"Where did you college?"

"NYU," she lied.

"That's a great school. How did you find your way here?"

She was prepared. She'd known she'd get the question one day or another. "Randal, you trusted me, and now I'll have to trust you. Okay?"

"Sure."

"It's hard to describe," she said. "I work for an outfit called Premium Choices. Ever hear of it?" He hadn't, and she explained. "They study people's split lives, their working lives in comparison to their time at home, and determine how one affects the other, and how people then see and evaluate their lives." She laughed. "I'm here to report how people at Saugatuck Investments match up what they do there with their personal lives. Which one wins, so to speak. I'm only at Saugatuck temporarily. I can't tell you how much you have helped me. I'll be sorry when I leave in a year and go someplace else."

"Golly," he said, and nothing more, and Kelsie didn't know whether he was impressed or unhappy that she wouldn't be around him permanently, and suspected it was the latter. She saw a chance to escape by rising and going to help a crying little girl rebuild a sandcastle that a boy had just maliciously wrecked and was more than relieved when Randal joined them.

Randal didn't ask any further questions, and after the sandcastle was built and the happy child had run off to her parents, they ate lunch, and drank the wine, and the day flew by.

The beach had started to empty when she

said, "I'm buying you dinner at that French place we ate at the other night, and afterwards we are going back to Saugatuck Investments."

"You really want to?"

"Yes." And she did. Their last hacking glimpse into the sex life of none other than Bellistree himself had produced something far more rewarding. As their laughter had begun to die over the Saugatuck Investments president's latest escapade with Pat Simmons, Kelsie had suddenly been seized by a thought.

"Wait," she'd said. "Perhaps it's only a hunch, but why is he playing around with Pat? Given his position, I'm sure there must be a half dozen far prettier girls who'd be willing to put up with his gross unattractiveness. And probably for a substantial job advancement."

"Getting inside investment information?"

"He doesn't need her for that."

"Then what else?"

There hadn't been an answer then. Both had been worn out from a long day, and today's picnic on the beach. But now, as they headed for her car, Kelsie knew there had to be a reason, and it could be seriously important.

"What about my car?" Randal had left it at the garage for repair, and Kelsie had picked him up there to go to the beach.

Kelsie firmly took charge. "It can wait until tomorrow. They're more than likely shut now anyway. You can taxi home."

Randal didn't argue.

Twenty-Seven

Randal's fingers flew, and in a moment they had a split screen, Pat Simmon's emails on one half, Bellistree's on the other. He slowly scrolled through what were obviously arrangements for office trysts already laughed over, and then suddenly Kelsie sat bolt upright and peered intently at the monitor.

"Look. That exchange. What does he mean with 'Let me know how it was handled?' and 'Did you put it in code?' That's not his being coy about their sex, Randal. Those have to be illegal disbursements they're talking about."

"You mean crooked stuff?"

"Yes. And if it's coded, then forget the 'how it was handled.' It sounds like it was possibly important stuff. Who does wire service?"

"Large disbursements would have to be Jake Pearson. Want to see?"

"Yes. Wouldn't you, if Bellistree is up to no good?"

"Sure. Hold on."

In what seemed but a few minutes, Kelsie

found herself looking into Jake Pearson's computer.

Randal said, "Nobody writes anything down anymore, so if he's sending stuff out, he's probably got it in a special file someplace."

Again there were dizzying images on the monitor screen that Kelsie could barely follow until suddenly it was all there in black and white. The date, then: $350,000 Chancellor Box Company; $400,000 Farnham Machine and Tool; $575,000 Pierson Carpeting.

"I'm going to look up those companies, Randal." She pulled his laptop closer and did it herself, one after another. And each seemed bona fide, although the sums disbursed to each were highly disproportionate to their normal gross in sales.

"Randal, they can't all three suddenly be having a surge in sales or income from investments. They're hiding something. Can we check the principals of each?"

Names came up at once: president, CEO, along with photographs. Each man looking like any corporate executive anywhere. Kelsie stared. They were meaningless.

She said, "Randal, pull up the website for the Western Patriot's Alliance," and when it quickly appeared, "Now its executive, if they're shown."

And in a second, she and Randal found themselves looking at photographs similar to those of the president and CEO of Chancellor Box Company.

Kelsie slowly let out her breath. "Jackpot," she said quietly, not just at this revelation but at another that accompanied it. The faces she saw were also familiar from seeing them at Melissa's party, with their names being written on the place cards on the dining tables next to the place cards that were blank. Paulstein's wife was in this, and just as she'd thought, in it more deeply than just getting her a job and putting her up at Soundview.

She got Randal to repeat the procedure with the two other companies. Images of their executives matched images of known white nationalist leaders.

Sitting back from the laptop, he said, "Same thing. I think we ought to call the FBI in on them."

"Not yet." Kelsie turned to look at him. He appeared truly shocked.

"But why not? Jesus Christ, Kels, this is criminal fraud from Bellistree on down. Saugatuck Investments—we're handing money to terrorists."

It was the moment, she knew, when she ought to tell him who she was and why she was there. But she couldn't bring herself to. In his lonely life, she had become a refuge from every sling and arrow, the only person Randal trusted and believed in. Telling him their ever warmer relationship, which clearly meant so very much to him, was a fraud, that it was business on her part, would be deeply hurtful betrayal, the worst.

The truth about her would have to wait until she could slowly ease herself out of his life, and that meant holding off notifying Washington of Bellistree and where the money was going.

Randal said, "I think you're wrong. I'm going to shoot them a message right now."

"You'll get yourself fired."

"Don't care."

"Randal." Sharply. "*Don't.* This is dangerous. We need to think how to do it so we avoid having nationalists after us and get ourselves burned on a cross somewhere. Randal, they murder people."

He looked and sounded momentarily set back. "Gosh. Well, maybe …"

She searched desperately for another excuse. She needed time, and said, "I'm right, and you know it. We need to think about this rationally. So sit tight a few minutes while I make a trip down the hall."

She flashed him a calming smile she didn't feel, and rose, and left him. She had just got into the restroom when the lights went out. And then, in the confused and surprised moment or two later as she fumbled about in the dark trying to remember where the light switch was, she heard the shot.

In the stillness of the empty building, it sounded like a cannon. When silence returned and her ears stopped ringing, questions began to race. What on earth was happening? Had the night watchman done something? A gas explosion? What?

Feeling her way in the inky darkness, she left the restroom and carefully felt her way down the hall, back to the research room, helped by a faint light from lamps in the parking lot below.

"Randal? What's happened? Randal?" And then any more words were silenced, and a startled gasp as she fell over him where he was crumpled on the floor just outside his cubicle. Rising, she felt sticky blood on her hands and knew there was blood on her face also. Fumbling in the darkness, she found her shoulder bag where she'd hung it over a chair, and fished out her cell phone, and turned on its light.

As she did, and as full sickening realization that Randal was very dead rushed over her, she hear the sound of a motorcycle starting, and then the sound fading as it left the parking lot and sped off down the nighttime road beyond it.

Twenty-Eight

She felt ill, like vomiting, and it was hard to breathe. Clutching the wrap-around shelf inside the cubicle, she just stood there, unable to move, hardly able to think. This wasn't Mohammed Adi, whom she hadn't known, or the sick hit man years ago in Brooklyn. This was Randal, whom she'd come to care about, someone who for a little while had erased some of the anger that was always there gnawing someplace deep inside her, someone who had made her feel a glimmer of hope. This was a gentle and giving person with a life ahead of him, someone who, for the first time in years, she had begun to feel she wanted to be intimately involved with.

The silence around her was the dead silence of a tomb until a falsely set digital alarm rang from a far corner of the room. Its brief musical note first jarred her with fear, then brought her to her senses when she realized what it was.

Almost reluctantly, she stepped away from Randal and felt a first rush of anger. The 500 cc sound of the motorbike was sickeningly familiar.

The killer had to be the same Grigori Lebedev who had killed Mohammed Adi. But why kill Randal?

That was when the terrifying realization finally struck. Randal wasn't meant to be the one killed, to be lying dead on the floor outside the cubicle. She was.

Her thoughts raced to add it up. Randal's car was in the garage for repairs. He'd taken a taxi to work, and she had driven him to and from the beach, to the restaurant, and then here. Hers was the only car in the parking lot below, and Lebedev had got onto its rental registration somehow, perhaps tailing her that morning from Soundview. And probably, she thought, he had previously conned the building and had noted, as a matter of course, where the master electric panel was. When he had seen light in the research area, he'd known where to cut the power and then where to go. And when reaching the cubicles, he had aimed at a shadowy figure only slightly illuminated by a streetlight in the parking area below.

She stood a moment, simply staring down at Randal, at the blood puddling around his head and shoulders and slowly making a small lake on the floor, at his dead staring eyes that only moments ago had been so full of dancing life.

Oh, my God, what had happened? Where was the night watchman? He was elderly and might have fallen asleep in his little watch station in the basement, where he had a comfortable chair to which he retired between his hourly rounds of the building to brew coffee and watch TV. Hadn't he heard the shot? Been aware when the lights had gone off? Had Lebedev silenced him somehow first? Was he dead also?

Reality came back in a cold and frightening rush. She had to leave. She grabbed her shoulder bag, and remembered that she was leaving Randal's laptop behind, with all the evidence of what she had just seen. She looked frantically for it, and when she didn't see it on the shelving of his cubicle where they had been using it, she wildly swung her cell phone light around, thinking it might have fallen to the floor. To her horror she saw it had. It had gone down with Randal as he fell and was half pinned under his body in a swamp of blood.

Everything in her froze for an instant until she bent to retrieve it, and found she couldn't. It was too wedged under Randal and too slippery with blood for her to get a grip on it and pull it loose. She tried to roll Randal off it and couldn't. His body was too wedged between his cubicle and an outside wall.

Fear overtook her again. She'd have to leave it, rely on the report she'd give Suarez, and perhaps she could find what she and Randal had just learned on her own, or the FBI could. She stepped over Randal's body into her own cubicle, and lifted her own laptop from where she'd left it on her shelf, and had turned to go when she remembered seeing a thumb drive on Randal's computer. Tonight's revelations wouldn't be on it; they'd been working together on his laptop as usual. but there could be something. Stepping over his body again, she went back into his cubicle, pulled the thumb drive, and shoved it into her jeans pocket.

She had to go, and fast, she knew. But for a moment she couldn't. She stared down through the darkness at Randal in a moment's silence in which, she remembered later, she could hear the running waters of the Saugatuck River break the dead silence. Then she said, suddenly feeling the deep pain of it and barely getting the whispered words out, "Good-bye, Randal, I'm so sorry, so terribly sorry," and realized she was crying. She bent and touched his body, then softly slipped away to cautiously and silently leave the building.

In her car, its doors locked, her hand clenching her Beretta, she was able, after a few moments, to add things up. It was Lebedev who had just killed Randal, she was sure of it. The sound of his 500 cc motorbike was seared in her memory. But who had put him on to her? Who had become certain she'd soon uncover disbursements of the Russian laundered money to various hate groups of white nationalists and had ordered her killing? Bellistree? She thought not. He might be able to talk his way out of financing hate groups—perhaps he'd blame it all on poor pathetic Pat Simpson—but he wouldn't want to be tagged as an accomplice to murder. Melissa? Perhaps, although she also found it hard to believe that she would take such a risk. Then who? She had no answer.

Then she began to wonder what she should do herself. Should she dial 911? She reached for her cell but stopped. Better not. She'd only find herself spending a long night at the police station, unmasked and perhaps it leaking out as to why she was there, and so blowing the whole investigation. Better to let someone coming to work discover Randal and, if he also had been killed, the night watchman too.

After a few more moments, she drove away, her mind made up. She couldn't return to "work" in the morning—the place would be in an uproar, with police and Forensic all over everywhere, the building even shut down probably, and more likely the police looking for her and assuming her guilt when she didn't show up for work as usual. She felt she had to sleep. She was exhausted, and Melissa was more than likely not going to hear what had happened at Saugatuck Investments until she rose, which was never before nine or ten.

She was done with the job anyway. She had enough evidence for FinCen to bring in the FBI and for the whole rotten operation to be closed down and arrests made, and it brought a faint smile to her face when she thought of Bellistree, and possibly even Melissa, up before a grand jury and eventually behind bars.

So it was back to Soundview. She'd put in her report to Suarez as soon as she got there, implicating both, then get Randal's blood off her hands, and if there was any on her clothing, change into something else. Her car clock said it was slightly past one a.m. She had time for a few hours' sleep if she didn't set her alarm until six. There were commuter trains both before and after that hour, so there was time to return the rented car and get herself to New York. With no planes after nine p.m., it would be the Amtrak to Washington instead.

Reaching the palatial Paulstein home, she turned off her car's lights, and drove slowly up the driveway, and parked behind the Bentley so as not to be seen from the house. She had only just started to get out of the car when the hall and front door lights suddenly went on, flooding the whole front of the house. Startled, and instantly feeling caught, she stopped short, using the big Rolls-Royce as a shield from being seen, and then was even more startled when a woman in a housecoat came out with a man. Was that the security guard who she'd been briefed was there at night to guard the millions of dollars of art treasures in the house?

Kelsie had hardly registered that it was Melissa with him, her normally severely coiffed hair in disarray and her face without a careful mask of makeup, when she saw, parked across the front driveway circle, something that in the dark she hadn't seen before—a heavy motor-cycle. And then, as the man with Melissa turned, framed in the bright light, she recognized the face and figure she could never forget. Everything in her froze. She eased her little Beretta from her shoulder bag, took off its safety catch, and waited for what seemed an eternity until Grigori Lebedev went to the bike, started it up, and with its motor rumbling, went slowly down the driveway.

Twenty-Nine

They think I'm dead, Kelsie said to herself. She hadn't moved from the protection offered her by the big Rolls since the sound of the motorcycle had slowly faded into silence and Melissa, back inside Soundview, had turned out the lights.

She remained rooted to where she was when the lights had first come on and Melissa had appeared. She felt completely unnerved by the revelation that Melissa was somehow intimately involved with Lebedev. And who else? Who had engineered the killing? She couldn't imagine Melissa being alone in it. Fear clutched at her like an icy fist. The motorcycle, the shot. The photographs Joshua Marshall had spread out on Suarez's desk. The horrid chinless jaw supporting a dirty little goatee, the thin almost nonexistent lips, the pale expressionless eyes. The tattoos.

She was living in a nightmare, and no longer thought of being seen. She only thought of what had happened at Saugatuck Investments; she thought only of Randal, and was surprised when she realized that she was crying. She hadn't for years. *He had a crush on me,* she thought. *That's what everyone said. And now I know how much I'd come to care about him. Oh, God, Randal, what has my existence done to you?*

Waves of guilt flooded over her. If only she hadn't agreed to his hacking fun; if only he hadn't garaged his car so that hers was the only one in the parking lot, making her presence obvious; if only bloody Grigori Lebedev, the horror, hadn't turned out the lights. If only …

For a few minutes she couldn't move. She just stood, feeling helpless. Then she slowly came to her senses. Yes, they didn't know she was alive, and for tonight at least, until the police swarmed Saugatuck Investments and Bellistree got hold of Melissa, or worse, came out to see her with the news, she was safe. Melissa had not once in three weeks come down the wing of the house to her room. And assured she was dead, surely would have no reason to do so now.

Deciding against any light at all, Kelsie kept her cell in her shoulder bag where it was usually stowed and made her way slowly to the door that, when she opened it, would let her enter the long corridor to the stairs that ended above in the hallway just outside her room.

There was a moon, and it helped. She kept her little Beretta at the ready, and inside she refrained from turning on the hall lights. Nor did she turn on lights when she had finally reached her room. She was lucky so far. Why test it? Inside, she locked her door, went into the bathroom, remembering that its window faced away from Melissa's section of the house but pulling down the shade, then drawing closed the heavy curtains before turning on the lights.

The first sight of herself in the room's mirrored walls was a shock. Looking back at her she saw a disheveled woman whose hair, face, and hands were covered with blood. Her shirt and jeans too. There was even some blood on one of her feet. She had fallen over Randal, she remembered, had landed on him and had struggled a moment to right herself and step away from his inert body.

She placed the Beretta carefully on a chair by the glass-walled shower, and got in under a hot spray, and washed all of herself, starting with her hair, using shampoo that was placed for guests along with the soap.

Shower finished, she donned a soft terry-cloth robe, dried her hair with the electric dryer hung next to the sink, turned off the light, and retrieving her Beretta, went back into the pitch-dark bedroom where, thinking ahead, she had left her cell on the bedside table. Carefully fumbling her way to it, trying as she went to remember the exact layout of the room so as not to crash into anything, she got to it and turned it on.

As she did she was startled and half-blinded by the room's overhead lights suddenly turning on at the same time. She blinked back the glare and found herself looking at Melissa Paulstein.

She was wearing the same expensive dressing gown she'd had on when seeing Grigori Lebedev to the door, and she had a handgun leveled.

She said silkily, and with a faint smile, "Grigori went back to get a clip he'd mistakenly dropped, and found he'd got the wrong person. He's on his way. He'll want you out of here, and so do I, so get dressed."

Gun in hand and overconfident, she reached into her robe pocket to get out her cigarette case, and in that one second when she took her eyes off Kelsie, Kelsie shot.

The bullet from the Beretta caught Melissa in the throat and she fell, twisting around on the floor and searching about blindly for her handgun, which had fallen with her. She reached it, swung it around, pointing, one finger searched the trigger, and Kelsie shot her again and without hesitation. And Melissa was still.

Kelsie knew she had little if any time. She threw on the bloody clothes she'd just taken off, ignored her suitcase, grabbed only her laptop and handbag, and went straight for the stair, then the corridor, that would exit her from the house.

Once down and turning off the corridor lights, she very quietly opened the door and looked out just as she heard first the noise of an approaching motorcycle, the crunch of the big bike's heavy wheels on gravel, and then silence with Lebedev dismounting and heading fast for the front door. He rang, then frustrated, rang again several times, and pounded and shouted.

The door suddenly opened. A maid appeared, in her bathrobe and confused by being woken from sleep. Grigori, shouting in Russian, pushed her roughly aside and went in.

Kelsie moved quickly. In seconds she was in her rented car, which she started and ran up alongside the motorcycle. Reaching out the window, she unscrewed its gas cap and poured in a half can of Coke she'd left in the holder on the between-seats console the day before, then screwed the gas cap back on. That done, she put on her headlights and took off down the driveway at speed.

She knew the roads by now, and drove fast through the town, hoping she wouldn't be stopped by a late-night cop. She was lucky, as none appeared, and she pulled to a quick stop before the car rental office in the parking lot of the rail station.

She found the office shut. She hesitated. If she went on with the car to New York, suppose Lebedev followed, commandeering one belonging to a Soundview employee, or more conveniently taking the big high-speed Rolls? If he caught up, he'd run her off the road or trigger off another shot. She dropped the keys into the drop box by the door and went to one of the taxis waiting for a pickup from people who might be coming on a late train from theater in New York. A taxi was anonymous.

She woke the driver. "When's the next train?"

"You've got about a twenty-minute wait."

"New York then, and fast," she said.

"Wait a minute, lady. I'm not going to New York."

"Yes, you are."

"Who says?"

"The U.S. Government."

"C'mon, lady, with that crap."

"Behind your wheel and now."

The driver found a Beretta handgun in his face. "And quick time. You'll see official ID when we start rolling."

He slowly obeyed.

Thirty

Joshua Marshall got the call on his bedside phone even before he'd risen. His wife, beside him in bed, rolled across him to pick up the receiver, and when the caller announced herself, she quickly shook her husband awake, and ignoring his muttered questions, handed him the receiver.

"Marshall."

"Josh, Marie Suarez. We have a problem. I want you in the office right away."

It was only four thirty a.m. Thirty minutes later, he parked his car outside the FinCen offices, almost glad of the hour. There had been almost no traffic at all, the Beltway and Virginia streets ghostly in their near emptiness. Punching five buttons on the keypad lock, he pushed the door open and took the elevator up to the floor housing Marie Suarez, himself, and other senior members of the FinCen criminal division.

After knocking on the door, he entered Suarez's office to find a tired Marie at her desk, waiting for him, along with Charles Wheeler, who looked as though he'd had a late night. But they weren't the only ones. Joshua came up short when he saw Kelsie Gordon, one of Marie Suarez's office cardigans thrown over her torn half-open blood-stained shirt, and wearing nothing else but jeans and sockless sneakers. She was clutching her laptop and her handbag as though to save both from a shipwreck, and was deathly pale.

And then Joshua saw a fifth person he barely remembered from previous meetings, an anonymous-looking expressionless guy, not young, not old, and in a business suit, who clearly hadn't yet shaved that morning.

A little taken back but hiding it, Joshua said, "Marie, Charles, good morning. Miss Gordon, what's up?"

Marie Suarez said, "A lot. Good and bad. The good is Miss Gordon's brung down the curtain on exactly who is getting the Russian money she's been chasing for six months. The bad is two deaths—one, another cold-blooded killing by our friend Grigori Lebedev, the other, Melissa Paulstein, shot dead late last night by Miss Gordon herself. We don't believe either body has yet been discovered. We don't expect much of an uproar over the one at Saugatuck Investments, but all hell's going to break loose when they find Mrs. Paulstein."

The anonymous-looking man rose and stuck out his hand. "Jim Thorpe, FBI, Mr. Marshall. Pleasure to see you again. I'm here only for a preliminary briefing."

Suarez said to Joshua, "A quick fill-in, Josh. Miss Gordon phoned me at one a.m. while in a taxi headed to New York. That was about an hour and a half after the murder at the Saugatuck Investments building, while she and the murdered man were unearthing who at Saugatuck was sending money and to whom. The killer was apparently the same Grigori Lebedev as the guy who killed Mohammed Adi.

"The second shooting, Miss Gordon's taking down Mrs. Paulstein, occurred only about forty-five minutes later when, apparently in cahoots with Lebedev, Mrs. Paulstein confronted her with a gun to await her being removed from the Paulstein home to be killed and disposed of someplace less incriminating by Lebedev, who was on his way to do just that. Kelsie's first shot took the Paulstein woman down but not out, and Miss Gordon had to shoot her again to stop her from recovering her gun, which would assuredly have meant her own death."

Joshua glanced at Kelsie. She returned his look with a surprisingly level one of her own and with no apparent emotion. It was as though nothing had happened, that she'd not been almost killed by Lebedev who, she guessed, got the wrong person, and then had triggered her own gun.

From all he'd heard of her from the venerable old deacon, he wasn't altogether surprised at her icy cool but he noticed she'd put a restraining hand on one of her legs, which was nervously tremoring. *Incredible that she's sane and human in spite of it all,* he thought.

Thorpe said, "Marie got me at three. I've alerted our people in Connecticut. They've already been over to the building. They got inside, found the night watchman groggy still from a blow on the head, and then the dead person upstairs, a relatively young man, half his head blown off."

"Computers?" Joshua said.

"We've already seized a lot of them. Particularly, at Miss Gordon's instruction, the laptop and computer belonging to a Mr. Bellistree, the company president and CEO, and those of a woman he was apparently intimate with, a Miss Simpson, in the investment department. We have hers and the dead man's also, and a third belonging to a Mr. Jake Pearson. The building was put on immediate lockdown the moment the body was discovered. Same for Soundview, the Paulstein residence. The local police were alerted and are assisting."

"What about the press?"

"Given the nature of the entire situation, we're putting an official lid on everything."

Suarez spoke, noting that Charles Wheeler hadn't said anything. "Charles, Melissa was your cookie. Can you explain her tie to Lebedev?"

"No, I can't, Marie. I'm as bewildered as anybody. I had no indication whatsoever she was playing a double game." He turned to Kelsie.

"According to your account, she had summoned Lebedev, and if so, wouldn't it have taken him some few minutes at least to get from the Saugatuck building to Soundview?"

"Probably ten or fifteen."

"You couldn't have held off, fled? You had a car."

Suarez bridled in defense. She said sharply, "Charles, Kelsie had a gun leveled at her."

"A gun doesn't sound at all like Melissa. I'm not disputing that Melissa had one, if that's what Miss Gordon says, but with all respect, I think her account needs reviewing. If she was at Lebedev's killing in the Saugatuck building, as she says, she might understandably have been too upset to judge Melissa correctly. I mean, could Melissa have been armed because she knew Lebedev was coming, and she was prepared to defend both herself and Miss Gordon? Or—a more likely scenario—because she heard Miss Gordon coming home, and due to the hour, thought it might be an intruder? Her home is a gold lode of jewelry and art."

Joshua was thinking Charles was the one misjudging when Kelsie answered in an unexpected explosion of anger. With no warning, she was suddenly on her feet, her whole body rigid, her voice nearly a scream.

"You stupid son of a bitch. That's laughable when a guy's dead because you're the one who misjudged Melissa Paulstein. And right from the beginning. She never was in your pocket, asshole. You were in hers. And don't tell me no. I was there. You were not. Randal Sherman is dead because of you. A wonderful innocent guy Lebedev had never heard of and who wasn't supposed to be his target when obviously I was."

The outburst took every one off guard, except Joshua. He was suddenly aware that he was unexpectedly seeing the home-life side of Kelsie, the woman described to him by the deacon. The Randal Sherman mistakenly shot at the Saugatuck Investments offices—she obviously was close to him, or becoming so.

He said, "She's right, Charles. But don't take it hard. We've all been double-agent fooled at one time or another."

Wheeler started to reply, "Come off it, Joshua. This isn't the SPLC …"

And was going to say more when Kelsie burst out again. "Fuck you, Charles. And go to hell."

Suarez jumped in. "Shut up, all of you. Miss Gordon, sit down, please. This meeting wasn't called to argue details. It was to make it clear to everyone what we're saddled with and the need for total secrecy. One word from anyone of Miss Gordon being responsible for Melissa Paulstein's death and I'll want to know why. The media, as far as every single one of us is concerned, for the moment doesn't exist. And I'm sure Mr. Thorpe agrees with me."

Jim Thorpe said quietly, "The FBI has already issued a departmental gag order and informed the office of the Connecticut governor. For the moment it will only be said that Mrs. Paulstein was apparently a suicide due to the intransigencies of her husband." He turned to Kelsie. "Miss Gordon, for just a moment before we go on, could you help me with one small detail that I'll need. What sort of gun is yours?"

"A Beretta APX."

"And I know it was pointed at you, but Paulstein's? Get a look?"

"Hers was a standard Glock Cutdown 26 or 27."

"Sharp eyes, considering. How about the man? Lebedev."

"I think Forensic will find it the same as used to kill Mohammed Adi. A .45 automatic."

"Thank you." Thorpe smiled. "I'm sure your take will verify whatever Forensic finds." And to Suarez, "Marie, that's all from me at the moment. I'll call you early this afternoon or sooner if I hear from Forensic before then."

Suarez said, "Meeting dismissed. Kelsie, don't plan to go anywhere other than where you live or directly here. Joshua, perhaps you could see Miss Gordon home?"

"Sure. Kelsie?"

She left with him and followed him down in the parking lot. When she sat in the front passenger seat of his car, Joshua felt as though he was sitting next to a ticking bomb about to go off. If there was any doubt about her story by anyone, he thought, it was dispelled by the utter nonsense Charles Wheeler had come out with.

You didn't deny the factual report of one of their own agents like that, especially given her record on the case before Saugatuck and the way she had weathered the Mohammed Adi shooting.

He was most of the way into Washington in the now morning rush hour before he sensed her relax a little, and dared ask a question.

"This poor fellow who got shot. Did you know him?"

A silence, then: "Yes."

Joshua sensed there was more. He waited and then tried again. "How well?"

"Very."

He heard a faint muffled sound and, glancing over at her, he saw her teeth clenched fighting back tears.

Not completely surprised, he said, "Didn't know that. That's tough, then. Sorry."

There was another silence, until from her: "It's okay. Just tired."

"Sure. You've had a long night. Did you work together?"

"Yes. Several weeks and then all our hacking."

"Anything gained that will specifically reveal who has been behind all this?"

"Possibly. I— We didn't get that far, but something might show up on the computers the FBI has seized."

They didn't speak then, either of them, until they reached her house and he'd pulled up to let her out.

Before she left the car, she said, and with a kind of sincerity he hadn't expected, "Thank you for the ride."

Joshua thought of all she'd been through long before this incident. He thought of her mother's funeral, and then her guardian's, and the burden she now carried with her brother's drug addiction, and keeping a home for him as well as for herself.

He said, "Pleasure. Great job you did."

He got a rare smile for his pains, and after he'd watched her go up the steps to her home and disappear inside, he drove away.

Thirty-One

The official review took place at FBI head-quarters in Washington, and its seriousness was emphasized by the presence among those attending of a high-ranking Treasury official as well as the head of FinCen and Marie Suarez's boss, Gregory "Mace" Armstrong, so nicknamed for his no-quarter tactics no matter what the problem. Also present was the FBI's Jim Thorpe, along with his superior in counterintelligence, Donald Wolkowski, Marie Suarez, and Joshua Marshall. Oddly absent was Charles Wheeler.

The relentless questioning of Kelsie began almost the moment the meeting was declared in order. It was as though she were the guilty one and not Melissa Paulstein. Endless and exhaustive questions probed her job record from the day she left the John Jay School of Criminal Justice to nearly every case she'd worked on while with the Brooklyn DA, and subsequently her every movement since she had come first to the FBI and then to the Treasury's FinCen. Most of it was aimed not just at exacting a detailed and sequential order to every event in the investigation in America of the Russian laundered money, in which she had a presence, beginning with the murder of the Saudi royal Mohammed Adi. It also was aimed at any hint she might have received, no matter how subtle, of leakage of information not just to herself but to others—Melissa Paulstein, Grisham, even Agnes the maid.

The FBI team wanted to know also every aspect and every moment of her days in Connecticut. It went on and on, and dug deeper and deeper, until virtually every inch of her stay there from her first night in a hotel to her hurried departure after the shooting was covered, in near microscopic detail.

There were questions demanding a complete description of the department she worked in at Saugatuck Investments, the names of as many employees as she could remember, and who she got along with and with whom she didn't. How did she like the boss, Bellistree, and especially what was her relationship with Randal Sherman, the other shooting victim?

Questioning too was arduous when it came to any and all of her communications with Wheeler himself in her association with him. Fortuitously, she had recorded his instructions to her, and they were played not once but several times, along with recordings of Wheeler's comments during meetings in Marie Suarez's office.

And there was much more. For over an hour

she was also questioned on all the talking and texting before the hacking she had done with Randal, and she suffered numerous questions not only about who he was and how safe she believed him to be—what were his dealings with Melissa, with Wheeler? Most painful of all to Kelsie was the endless cold questioning about Randal's and her personal relationship. "Describe your dinners together." "Why your car and not his?" Were they intimate? Had she ever known him before? How much did they work together? Did she ever reveal why she was there?

And, of course, every moment of his being shot, from the moment the lights went out— Where was she? Where was he?—to her falling over his body, and the sound of the motorcycle disappearing into the night, with her belief it was the same motorcycle from which its rider had shot Mohammed Adi. It made her realize that for one of the very few times in her life, she had fallen in love with someone, and that if it had not been for his death, their relationship unquestionably would have become permanent. There were moments when she felt too shattered and heartbroken to speak.

Finally there was her shooting Melissa Paulstein: "Any personal relationships with the victim prior to killing her?" "What was the precise time?" "How far away from the victim were you standing?" "Did you reload for the second shot?" "Did you have prior indication of what your say was her guilt?" "Why did you go to your room when you had just seen her with the killer?" "Were you at all aware before she appeared that she might do so?"

When the day finally came to an end and Marie Suarez had herself and Kelsie driven away from FBI headquarters in a Treasury Department car, Suarez said, "Don't take it hard. They were doing the same to you as they do to one of their own. A lot of words that come to nothing, except that once in a zillion years, when they don't do it, they get caught when it turns out they've missed a killer in their own ranks, and it brings holy hell down on them from everywhere, especially from the White House and the media."

She had the car drop Kelsie off at her home and advised her, "Have a drink. Relax. Take tomorrow off," and then with a laugh, "Too bad you didn't shoot the bitch three times, not just two," and was gone.

Kelsie went up the steps to her front door. She felt exhausted, and thought, *I'm going to do just what Suarez said. I'm going to collapse and get drunk.*

It wasn't to be. She got out the words, "Gareth? Are you home?" and anything else was choked off in a gasp. What she saw when she stepped inside and closed the door behind her was worse than a nightmare. Her home had been ransacked. The kitchen table was turned over, along with its chairs, pots and pans were strewn about, glassware shattered on the floor.

In the living room, books had been dumped from now bare bookshelves, her few liquor bottles, normally discreet on a side table along with glasses and an ice bucket, were thrown around, the couch overturned, and amid it all, the framed photo of Angel lay among papers from the desk, its frame broken and its glass shattered.

Numb, Kelsie went to the minifridge in the living room and found a bottle of vodka. She brought it back, retrieved an unbroken glass on the floor and poured herself a double shot, and then fell on the couch.

Revenge, she thought. *Some fucking sonofabitch is getting theirs back at me.* And then *Who? Bellistree? He had to be under police surveillance in Connecticut. Lebedev? No. Lebedev didn't ransack, he shot. One of the bastard white supremacists I unearthed? No. None of those.*

She'd sat for some moments, wondering, when she suddenly realized who. The thought chilled. Charles Wheeler? Had to be. Who else was so intimately aware of her role in the case as to know where she lived? Whose game had she probably upset? Who was the only one of all who was nearby? And he hadn't showed up at the meeting today. Wrecking her home instead? It was as good a guess as any.

Still visualizing Wheeler with his silly bow tie, his preppy clothing and snobbish professorial air, she got out her cell and punched Gareth's number, relieved when he answered.

"Gareth. I'm back."

"So soon?"

"Not soon enough. I want you home."

"Can't. Got a date."

"Break it."

"Not about to. See you tomorrow night."

"No, you won't. You'll find the locks changed and yourself looking for a new place to live."

"Jesus. What the hell are you angry about now?"

"You'll see."

She clicked off, and went and poured herself another drink, careful as she did not to touch anything. Forensic would be coming in the morning, if not before, looking for prints, DNA, or whatever. She hoped she wouldn't be too knocked out to tell Gareth when he showed up.

Thirty-Two

lex Woodcott had been at his desk for an hour when he heard Marie Suarez call him. It was seven fifteen. He hadn't expected Suarez so early. She had called him at home around eleven in the evening and said she would be getting in late.

When he left his desk and went into her office, he found her shuffling papers and looking more severe than usual.

"Did you call Forensic?"

"Yes, ma'am. About half an hour ago. And Miss Gordon phoned just before you came in."

"And?"

"She said she'd be here right away. Had personal problems."

"I can well imagine. Given what she went home to. She called me late last night. And Wheeler?"

"I haven't been able to reach him. Neither his cell nor his landline answer."

"Email? Texting?"

"Same."

"Alex, do you think, as I do, that there might be a reason he wasn't at yesterday's meeting?"

"Yes, ma'am, I do. If nothing else, this is one hell of a strange moment for him to be off any contact."

Suarez punched in a number on her cell. When it answered, and she was identified as a caller, she listened a moment, then said, "The mess. Yes, I think so too. Code Red, regrettably. If it turns out we're wrong, so much the better."

She listened a moment, then clicked off and turned to Woodcott. "I think we're both right about Wheeler. FBI's Thorpe and others can't reach him. It seems inconceivable that Wheeler is a double. And right here in our office. But if he is, he could prove a valuable source of information. I still believe there's a connection he possibly could verify between Lebedev and Sokolov, and that Sokolov hasn't necessarily engineered the whole laundering himself. I know he's made a dozen trips over here recently, but he's one of those guys who is too smart to let himself be nailed for anything. He always dumps his responsibility on others."

"Bellistree?"

"Maybe someone bigger. We need to look more closely at white nationalists."

Alex agreed. "If the bureau can wade through diplomatic immunity to get him, and he talks, yes, we could learn a lot."

A small light lit up on Suarez's intercom phone.

"That's Gordon now. She's in the building."

Woodcott left, and a moment later Kelsie appeared.

Suarez said immediately, "Miss Gordon, did Forensic come?" She waved at a chair.

Kelsie remained standing and said, "Yes. About an hour ago. They'd already found a mess of odd prints when I left that weren't Gareth's or mine. They're probably Wheeler's."

"Wheeler's. You think so? Why?"

Her answer was a who-knows shrug.

Suarez sighed. "Well, Thorpe's after him. So one way or another, we'll find out. Okay for that. Now, ripping up your home. That did it for me. I'm requesting the DOJ to have their U.S. Marshals put you on witness protection. You and your brother both. Last thing we want is some sort of hostage situation with him being used as leverage."

"Sorry. We don't want protection."

Taken aback, even startled at the emphatic negative, Marie fumbled a moment for words. She looked hard at Kelsie, reminding herself that this was the same young woman who had come to her office only a day ago in a near state of exhaustion, her clothes bloodstained, to collapse on her couch.

She finally found her voice and said, "No? Why not? Miss Gordon, for God's sake, and forgive me if I call you Kelsie—haven't you had enough of these people? Lebedev is still loose. FBI hasn't checked him out of the country, although he could have slipped the border to Mexico or Canada. He's resourceful enough to hike woods or desert where there are no immigration safeguards, and he's clearly nuts. Who knows from whom he's getting his orders, back in Moscow or elsewhere? You are carrying a lot of information in your head that could be lethal to a number of people. I see you as being in acute danger."

"Probably. But I don't want protection."

"And your brother?"

"Gareth's just finishing school. And he needs to prep this summer for medical school next fall. He doesn't want interruptions."

Suarez half-smiled. "You sound like a mother. But look, whatever his schedule, it can be handled. We can easily arrange for prepping someplace he could disappear to and where he'd be surrounded by people. New York, say? He knows it. He was with you in school there when you worked for the DA in Brooklyn. How about NYU or Columbia?"

A silence, then, "Him, but not me."

Saurez said, "Well, okay, you're making some half sense anyway. And I'll see he's bothered the least amount possible." She paused and said, "Now back to you. I can't fathom your reason, but if you don't want it, you don't, and that's that. Meanwhile, there's your job to discuss. I'm calling it. Consider yourself on paid leave with full benefits for a month."

"Sorry, as far as I'm concerned, I'm still working."

Another refusal. Suarez barely managed to hold down mounting exasperation. "Kelsie, let's get something straight. I'm the one here who makes decision, okay? This particular job you've been on for six months doesn't exist anymore. You've completed it. And I'm taking you off the active list whether you like it or not."

Kelsie shrugged. "You can do what you want, ma'am, but I lost someone to this crowd who had come to mean a lot to me, and I'm not quitting until I find out who was responsible. Lebedev was not really the hand that pulled the trigger. Nor the Paulstein creature."

Marie Saurez had a vague feeling that her agent also suspected Sokolov, but for some reason wasn't saying so. She realized she was getting nowhere, and inwardly sighed in resignation.

She said, "Suit yourself, but officially, you're on hold," and thought, *Let the chips fall.*

Thirty-Three

Charles Wheeler checked his Saudi passport, made possible by royal order in return for the extensive work he had done for the kingdom. Lately, that had included negotiating then arranging for passage of Russian money to come through a Riyadh bank as an additional move to confuse whomever might be tracing it.

Satisfied that his two other passports, one German, the other American, were in order, he pulled two letters from an envelope and scanned them quickly. Both were authorization as well as requests to afford the bearer, Mr. Charles Wheeler, every accommodation he found necessary to accomplish whatever mission, and to eliminate any bureaucratic steps normally required in order to expedite the request. Both were signed and officially stamped by high-ranking officials, in the case of the Saudi, a second in line to the crown prince and stamped with the Saudi royal seal.

They were letters Wheeler had obtained from the signatories by the simple and time-worn expedient of blackmail. In one, the signatory was guilty of fraudulently lining his pockets with large sums from a royal bank, which could well have caused his execution; in the other, with the signatory's infidelities. Putting them back in the envelope, he sealed it and secured it deep in his carry-on suitcase, which he then shut and locked before making what he hoped would be his final phone call in the States.

"Charles Wheeler. I'm leaving Washington in about two hours. Lebedev blew my cover, implicating me as well as Melissa, who was foolish enough to jump the Treasury agent we had to accept, and who unfortunately took Melissa out. Worse, she pillaged every computer in sight at Saugatuck and turned them over to the FBI. I assure you, however, that Nero is still completely secure, and I'll contact him once I'm in Riyadh. Sokolov too."

Clicking off, he thought how annoying it was that he had to leave. Everything was going smoothly until that fool Grigori Lebedev shot the wrong person at the Saugatuck Investment Company.

Giving a final check to his two-room Watergate apartment, he cursed Melissa for losing her head, and ignoring all the strict warnings about avoiding Gordon like the plague, and taking things into her own hands rather than letting him handle it. Well, she'd paid for it, the stupid bitch, by getting herself shot—she had everything any woman could ever want and hadn't been content to leave things be.

Worse among her sins was that the FBI, given that she'd been shot by a Treasury agent, would now be swarming Soundview, and they were bound, sooner or later, to come across evidence tying him also to Lebedev as well as revealing the double role he'd been playing. Bloody fools, both her and Lebedev, but that was the risk you always took when dealing with inferior people, no matter what sort of leverage you had to keep them in line.

He locked up the apartment, and downstairs had the doorman hail a cab, with orders to take him to Reagan National. Arriving, he checked into business class on a Saudia 787 flight to Riyadh, spent a half hour in the VIP lounge, having a drink and enjoying what would be his fortunate escape. It never would have been possible without yesterday's emergency meeting, called by Suarez, which had warned him right there and then to cut his losses and leave.

When the flight was ready to be called, Wheeler made his way to the gate. He was just showing his American passport and boarding pass prior to boarding when he found someone at his side, and another person who, standing in his way, flashed an ID.

"You'll come with us, please, Mr. Wheeler."

Thirty-Four

Close to finishing the job of putting their home back together again, Kelsie was mopping the kitchen floor when Gareth came down from putting things right in the bedrooms. He didn't have exams that day, and both he and Kelsie had slept late.

"Kels, what's this?" He held out his hand. "It fell out of a pocket in your jeans when I was dumping them into the laundry basket."

Kelsie half-looked. "It's a thumb drive."

"Yeah, I know. From your laptop?"

"Don't think so." She couldn't remember ever having taken any thumb drives with her. She rarely ever used them, and then only with her computer.

She'd gone back to straightening and cleaning up the kitchen when she suddenly remembered. It came flooding back to her like a giant slow-moving wave of dark ocean she couldn't run from and escape.

Herself standing frozen with fear in the silent darkness by hers and Randal's computers.

Her trying to get a fix on what to do. Was she alone, or was the killer still around? And deciding—get out and get out fast, in case he came back, or perhaps had already, and she hadn't heard, and he was there somewhere in the darkness and frightening silence. Then, at the last second, taking a chance and turning on her cell phone light and trying to free Randal's laptop, and giving up, and grabbing her own laptop and shoulder bag, and then, even without thinking, seeing the thumb drive on his computer and shoving it in her jeans pocket. Blindly but with no real thought at all. Only some vague idea that it might hold something important.

And then, unaware of it again in the confrontation with Melissa, and afterward on the ride in the taxi to New York and the flight to Washington, when she had avoided the stares of other passengers and the flight attendant asking her how she'd got blood all over her shirt.

Until now. Her head buzzed. Was there anything of importance on it? Until she played it, she wouldn't know. But with Gareth home from school, and her now free from work, she wasn't going to allow anything related to her experience at Saugatuck Investments ruin her chance to spend time with him.

"Gareth," she said. "You deserve a drink for finding it."

"Do I get to pour it?"

She laughed. "This time only."

They finished work, and collapsed in the

living room, and while they slowly drank and talked, Gareth tried to find out what was on the thumb drive. Or more or less did. Getting anything but superficial nonfacts from his sister, he'd long since learned, was like pulling teeth. But he decided to use the thumb drive as a way of getting other information from her.

"Do you know what's on it, or just guessing?"

"I told you. I won't know until I review it. Probably stuff related to the case I was on."

"What was the case all about?"

"Dishonesty."

"By whom?"

"A lot of people."

He tried another score of questions, but those first few were about as far as he could get. She wasn't having any more. Her life with Gareth was one thing. It was family and love and anxiety and caring. Her life at work was dirt and hate and duplicity. To her relief, he eventually gave up and submitted to her questions about his lacrosse team.

When he finally went off on a date, Kelsie had almost forgotten the thumb drive again. But when she remembered, she went straight upstairs and to the small table in her bedroom that served as her desk when home. And when she'd stuck the thumb drive into her own computer, and began to examine its contents, she quickly saw that it did indeed register hacking Randal had done, not investment research.

It was hard for her to do. One thing after

another made her feel that Randal was right there doing it with her, and she kept thinking, as the thumb drive unveiled his hacking, *If only I hadn't agreed to join him in doing it. If only we'd gone in two cars that night, and if only we hadn't gone back, but I'd let him drive me straight home to Soundview. If only …*

At first, all she saw were emails of fellow researchers whom he'd hacked before he and she had conspired together. Disappointed, she was nearly ready to eject the thumb drive when something suddenly caught her eye, on a PDF that at first appeared to be meaningless scribbles. She let it go by, but then thinking it just *might* be something, and determined not to miss anything, she backed up and took a second look.

It seemed to be writing, perhaps, although blurred. She stared, enlarged it, stared some more. The scribbling slowly began to make sense, until she finally realized that what she was seeing was loosely scrawled Russian. To her totally untutored eye, it amounted to perhaps two full phrases or sentences.

Surprised, she wondered for an instant why on earth Randal had been getting a message in Russian, then realized it had to be something he'd hacked from someone else's computer. Working with sudden intense interest, she traced it to Bellistree. Her thoughts jumbled. Did Bellistree speak Russian? Surely not. Wheeler did, she knew. Was it something from or to him? It looked as though the sender was Russian, but the recipient? What it might be was beyond her.

And then she chided herself for being stupid and breaking her head to find out. There was an easy way. Her computer could easily do it for her. She copied the Russian, fed it into a search engine, and asked for an English translation.

And in a few fast seconds, she found herself reading first the very blurred name of the sender, Sokolov, then two recipients, Wheeler and Bellistree. And finally the short message. "All future contacts change VP code name from Nero to Caesar."

The VP code name? The VP? Many things came slowly together. Sokolov and Bellistree both visiting Troutlake, the VP's fishing hideaway in Maine, the VP a longtime client of Saugatuck Investments. VP could only mean the vice president. Who else?

She tried to add it up more clearly, to make herself face and accept the awful truth: her father's racist outbursts at Angel, his duplicity in hiding his affair with her mother from the world, and hers and Gareth's birthright, so carefully hidden as well.

Nero was her father. And all the thinking about him had been wrong. He wasn't innocently and naively risking American secrets, as everyone thought. Or laying himself open to blackmail when president. Or allowing his foreign policy thinking to be persuaded in Putin's favor. It was the other way around. He'd been using his office, with all its political power, to persuade

Sokolov to secretly put up the billions laundered to Connecticut. To finance white supremacist organizations in sowing hate and divisiveness, to Russia's advantage.

Her vice president father, soon to be president, was the guiding force helping to engineer America's destruction.

Thirty-Five

Wheeler's arrest brought about an immediate shutdown of any released information from the intelligence community. Intelligence and counterintelligence officials met at both the Treasury and the FBI to discuss and analyze all of Wheeler's contacts, dating back years before he had worked for the government, and Kelsie, among the many interviewed, was questioned extensively again by the FBI, which, along with the CIA, had promptly initiated damage control.

To whom Charles actually owed loyalty was summed up by Marie Suarez in a last meeting with her staff only.

"He owed loyalty to nobody," she said. "Not to us, not to the Russians or the Saudis or Chinese, for that matter, or to whomever. In spite of all his elitist Ivy League nonsense, he was a completely free agent willing to do dirt for anyone who would pay enough. We had in our midst a person with absolutely no moral core whatsoever.

"On one hand he was working and well paid to see that white supremacist groups got the loot, and on the other, as his cover, working with us to expose them. Who knows what the FBI bunch might have on the bastard other than his tour with us? Or whatever handy stipend he might have raked off from Sokolov's billions. Or the same from the Saudis as the billions passed through their banks. Jim Thorpe told me nothing of the FBI's suspicion weeks ago, and I doubt he'll reveal anything now."

Throughout, Kelsie kept what she had learned on the thumb drive to herself, and planned to surrender it to no one. She was not altogether surprised by what she had unexpectedly read, a revelation that had evaded her and everyone else for so long. Its few damning words seemed almost natural in a sequence of events that had for her come to an end when she'd been forced to flee Soundview after her confrontation with Melissa Paulstein.

What the thumb drive revealed was not only a threat to her anonymity in her professional life but also a serious danger to personal plans she had where her father was concerned, which had nothing to do with governmental justice. It was only a question of days before the FBI analysts would pick up the PDF from Randal's computer itself, and she had to act before then, because when they did, she would be effectively blocked.

While maintaining her usual cold and standoffish manner officially, she had decided that she needed to prepare Gareth for what she planned. His graduation came only two days after Wheeler's arrest and was followed the day after by his twenty-first birthday, and to celebrate, Kelsie took him out to a fancy birthday dinner with five of his friends, and showered him with presents.

The day after, with all the celebrations finally over and Gareth home alone with her, she decided to start by letting him know what she'd been doing for a living the past six months.

"Gareth, there's something I need to tell you."

"What?"

"You're temporarily under federal protection."

"Wait a minute, I'm what?"

"Being protected by U.S. Marshals from the DOJ. You've been doing too much celebrating to notice, but you have a security detail protecting you, like the Secret Service. Look around. You'll see them: expressionless men hanging out wherever you go. Later, you'll possibly be getting a name change and a move to another city for prepping and for medical school."

"Kelsie, what the hell are you talking about? Protecting me from what, for Christ sake?"

Kelsie went and slowly poured herself a drink, mentally crossing fingers. How was Gareth going to take this? Would it set him off into a new round of addiction? Would she have to live with unrealistic anger for weeks, and worse, perhaps forever, their relationship destroyed?

She finally broke an uncomfortable silence.

She said, as quietly and calmly as she could, "Gareth, you've always badgered me to know what I was doing, so brace yourself. Here it is."

And then she told him. The whole story, from the time she arrived in Connecticut and checked into a hotel, her meeting Melissa and putting up at Soundview, her going to work at Saugatuck Investments, then hacking with Randal until the awful moment when in the inky darkness of the nighttime-empty office building Randal was shot. Her terrified flight then, when the sound of the motorcycle starting up and leaving the parking lot told her who the shooter actually was, her seeing him later at Soundview, and then her confrontation with Melissa that followed.

He was silent until she finally finished by telling him about bullying the cab driver at the station to take her to New York. "I had to hold a gun on the poor guy to get him to agree, but he finally loosened up and it was okay." She laughed. "Gave him a not-so-tall story to tell his grandchildren."

She waited until Gareth spoke. "And the guy in the office building, he meant to shoot you and got Randal instead?"

"He shot where he thought I was, yes."

"And then you shot this Melissa woman?"

"Self defense, yes. I've been cleared."

"You shot her twice?"

"I had to make sure."

"Jesus, Kels." Gareth again fell silent a few

moments, and then said, "How long have you been doing it? I mean, shooting people."

Kelsie managed a laugh. "You're making me sound like a killer. The answer is only once before. Back in Brooklyn. A Mafia thug. Same situation, him or me."

"All these years? You could have told me."

"I could have, yes. But you already had enough on your plate."

"We've never had secrets."

"I know."

Another long moment until Gareth said, "What else? You're holding something back. I can tell."

"You're right, but I'm not holding it back." She took a deep breath. "It's this. I'm going to see our father."

Thirty-Six

A deathly silence. And then Gareth's expression and tone when he spoke were of complete incomprehension, as though he hadn't heard her.

"See our father."

"Yes."

"You know who he is?"

"Yes."

"And never told me?" And when she didn't answer, he blurted out, "Why the hell not? And how did you find out? Who was he?"

"Is still. Not was."

It was too much for Gareth. He just stared.

Kelsie waited a moment and then said, "Gareth, brace yourself. This is going to be a shock. Your father, my stepfather, is a well-known public figure who spent a small fortune, I guess, hiding that he had illegitimate children, you and me, by our mother, who wasn't his wife."

Gareth made a visible effort not to be overwhelmed and to calm the rising anger at her having kept it a secret. He said, "Okay. So, you found out who we have for a father. I'm not going to ask you how you did, just, again—who the hell is he?"

Kelsie thought, *It's now or never*, and said bluntly, "He's Emanuel Arthur. The vice president."

Gareth's anger vanished, and he half laughed in disbelief. "Who?"

"Emanuel Arthur."

Incredulity again, "That son of a bitch who's soon to be president?"

"Yes."

Gareth rose, and went and renewed his drink, and came and sat next to her. It was a few moments before he broke the silence. His voice was calm. "Jesus Christ, the bloody VP. Kels, how long have you know this?"

"Since you were in elementary school."

"Why didn't you tell me?"

"You were just too young, for a start. And I was frightened that someday he'd do to us what he did to Angel just to keep us secret. But I'm telling you now, finally, because I can't go on living a lie any longer, and I'm going to face him up, and it will come out. I didn't want you to know about him from others. I felt you had to hear it from me first."

"You said, *did* to Angel. Like what?"

"He had her murdered."

"Jesus, Kels. He what?"

"There was no proof, but everybody knew. Angel was a real danger to him. She was the one person who could reveal who he was and what he was doing. And that leads me to tell you something else you don't know. It's more than confidential, Gareth, it's a government top secret. Blab it to anyone and you could be in serious trouble. I mean that. It could cost you your life. And mine with you, okay?"

She took a deep breath and said, "Our evangelical puritan holier-than-thou father, who has sworn an oath to uphold every law and value of the country he serves, as well as his church, this father of ours, if not guilty of treason, could well be close to it. He's certainly broken a lot of laws. It's what your big sister was doing in Connecticut. I tracked him down. Treasury and the FBI now have all the evidence, and his days as vice president are numbered."

Gareth couldn't find words to reply. He muttered, "Jesus, Kels," again and slumped weakly down on the couch.

Kelsie fixed up his drink, and sat down next to him, and put an arm around his shoulder. She said, "Gareth, love, I've been playing mother to you ever since Angel left us. That stops, and right now. I'm not your mother, I'm your sister, and you're a big guy out with all the girls and off to Medical School to become a doctor. I'll always be here for you, in your corner, if and when you should need me. You know that. But you're on your own from here on. I have do what I have to do, and I hope you respect that."

She shrugged and was silent, and then

because Gareth seemed to have understood and digested the news she'd sprung on him, and was no longer angry, she said, "I'm going to blow the whistle about you and me. I can't stand living a lie and in secret any longer. I'm going to force him to publicly admit his parentage."

Gareth nursed his drink until he said, "When and where do you plan to do that?"

"In Washington. At his home in the official vice president's house. Number One Observatory Circle. It's by the Naval Observatory on the outskirts of Georgetown. His wife is hosting a reception there next week. In three days. I plan to be one of the guests."

"Why there?"

"Because the next day he's leaving on a tour of Africa, and before then he's either at the White House or at home with just his wife, and I couldn't possibly justify showing up. If there's a reception and lots of people, I can."

"But what's the rush? Can't you wait t until he gets back from Africa?"

"No. He won't be back from Africa for ten days, and then it will be far too late."

"But why?"

"Because. Sorry." Kelsie's insides knotted. It was a fair enough question, and he was suddenly a very grown-up man, and not a little boy any longer. His acceptance of all she'd loaded on him was a relief to her beyond words, but just the same she didn't dare take him so far into her confidence as to answer that.

She had deliberately held back Randal's thumb drive, with its damning information implicating their father, in order to give herself time to do what she had to—for herself and for him. But the time had already passed where withholding it made sense. The FBI would already be very near to finishing a pillage of Randal's computer, if they hadn't already, and would almost certainly have the damming PDF in their hands. An arrest of her father was imminent, perhaps in a matter of days, and that would mean that her chances of getting anywhere near him in the foreseeable future would be nigh impossible.

She put it to bed then, and assumed a look, for Gareth's benefit, as though she'd lose her temper if he asked one more question. But long after he'd turned in, and even after she'd gone to bed herself, she found sleep difficult. She still had much to do right here in Washington and would be away tomorrow.

She had to see the dear old deacon who had conducted Angel's funeral service and had rounded up a gospel choir to help. She needed to go to the bank and make arrangements for Gareth to share her account. She needed to see their lawyer, and also had to add a handwritten letter to the documents she had in a safe deposit vault, and leave the vault key for Gareth. Among those documents were letters from Gareth's mother explaining her long-ago affair with his father. Others concerned legal property rights she had turned over to Angel, along with her will when she died, and Angel's will also that deeded the property to both her and Gareth.

Then, before she fell asleep, and with all her plans made, she found herself thinking about Randal, seeing him the way he had been at dinner, telling her about his dreams, or when close by her side he had excitedly showed her how he hacked. Her very last thought was how much she had started to love him, and with her telling him silently that what she was going to do was for him too.

Thirty-Seven

On a particularly run-down street in the worst crime-ridden section of east New York in Brooklyn, there was a store sandwiched among others on a dark and trash-littered narrow street that also ran past shut-down houses and low brownstone buildings. Announced by a faded sign over the door that said simply MIKE'S TIRES, it sold recapped and retreaded tires, piles of which were stacked willy-nilly on the sidewalk, with many spilling out onto the street itself.

Mike, who owned and operated the place, was in keeping in appearance with his surroundings, and one who lived daily with crime and criminal surroundings. Swarthy Italian in build, with unkempt thick dark hair and badly needing a shave, he was daily clothed in heavily oil-stained and rarely washed coveralls that partially hid a once brightly colored sweater touting Disneyland.

The day was hot, and a clouded sky threatened rain. Two days after Kelsie Gordon unloaded the truth of her basically anonymous life at Treasury to her brother, Mike himself stood in the darkened doorway of his store that was lit by only one unshaded hundred-watt bulb hanging by its cord from the ceiling. Finishing a beer, which he casually threw onto the already littered sidewalk, he watched disapprovingly as his helper, Guido, of mostly equal appearance, wrestled unaided a large truck tire toward a silently waiting truck, against the overly graffiti decorated side of which the two truckers casually leaned while smoking and drinking canned sodas.

One of the truckers, catching Mike's eye, nodded at someone down the street, and Mike, coming to life and looking, saw to his surprise a young woman approaching. Dressed conspicuously in a light summer frock, with her handbag slung casually over one shoulder and carrying a rolled-up umbrella, she seemed utterly unafraid, as she came closer, either of the neighborhood or any of the wolfish stares and whistles she collected from other store owners and especially from some teen gang members playing stickball.

Seeing Mike, she waved, and with an openly astonished smile breaking his face, Mike straightened up and waved back. "Kelsie!"

"Hi, Mike."

To the open surprise of the two indolent truckers awaiting Guido with the tire, Mike stepped forward to greet Kelsie, who unabashedly returned his warm embrace and welcoming kiss planted squarely on her forehead.

"What the fuck are you doing here, girl?"

Mike shouted, and before she could answer, ordered Guido to "get the lead out, and run down to the bodega, and grab back a couple or more beer." And to Kelsie again, "Heard you was down to Washington."

"Was and am," she said. "I took off a day to come and see you."

"No shit, sweetheart. Came to see old Mike? Well, well. And you all big time now, I heard."

"Not big time, Mike. Just a working girl, as always."

"As always, my ass. You wasn't doing no working girl stuff when you saved me from a fifty-years stretch, or maybe even the fry chair, when they had me up before the judge. So who are you rescuing now?"

Kelsie took out her wallet and flipped it open to show her Treasury Department badge. "The U.S. of A., or trying to."

Mike looked. "Wow! Holy fucking smoke. Sweetheart, that's big, big time." He abruptly seized Kelsie by the waist and effortlessly hoisted her upon a stack of tires to sit, and then sat up himself on an adjacent pile.

Kelsie laughed and said, "Mike I came up to ask a small favor."

"So spill it, sweetheart. Anything." He stabbed at his chest with one thick tire-dirty finger. "Here. That ticker in here. Tear it out if you want it. It's yours, okay?"

Kelsie took hold of his hand to hold it in hers and said, "Billy Gambetta. Is he still around?"

"Yeah. Sure. Saw him just last week. Looking same as ever, the sneaky bastard. Always reminds me of one of them weasel animals."

"Is he still working?"

Mike nodded at Kelsie's handbag. "You mean doing stuff?" And when she nodded, "Yeah. Mostly Mafia, and night and day, apparently. Heard he just did a big passport job for one of the dons, along with other stuff. You know who I mean. Alonzon, who's took over Premini's old crowd when Premini finally kicked. Do you need a job done? Billy still owes me for half a dozen tires he never paid for, and only stupids don't pay up to Mike."

"I need an ID and a letter."

"That thing in your wallet you showed me. That ain't good enough?"

"'Fraid not."

Guido arrived with a bag with half a dozen cold beer. Mike took the cap off two and handed one to Kelsie. Fresh in his mind as he did, was the long dangerous effort she'd made when while working with the DA she'd helped to bring down the Bertucci mafia crowd, especially their hit man, Carlos, who had done the two killings he'd been falsely accused of. She'd gone all the way underground for a while, and wearing a wire, had gathered evidence on Bertucci himself that had put the son of a bitch behind bars for a lifetime stretch, when posing as an illegal Finnish immigrant who couldn't speak English.

He said to Kelsie, "I'll need pictures."

"I brought some." She fished about her handbag and came up with several. Mike saw her Beretta as she did, and laughed, "See you're still toting that thing. Ever use it again?"

She gave him a long level look. "I'm saving it for someone."

Mike thought back to her being discovered by Bertucci's Carlos and having to shoot him. He'd cornered her in a bathroom and was pulling his gun when she beat him to it with hers. One single shot, bang, through his chest, just like that, and had walked out of Bertucci's house like all she'd done was mop the floor and work was finished for the day. Everyone in Brooklyn was still talking about it.

He said, "Know something, kid? You gotta be one in a million, and I love ya for it." And pulled her close for a hug. "But you're seething inside, burnin' up over something. I can tell. Nobody fools Mike. So, lemme give you a word, sweetheart, you probably don't need. Them things like you got tucked away in your bag, they ain't never no good for revenge or nothin' like that. Revenge gets you nothin'. Get it and you still get eat up. So don't you never go and use it if you can get by without, know what I mean?"

Kelsie nodded, kissed his cheek, and they sat a while in silence, drinking their beers, until Mike said, "Okay, sweetheart, come back maybe tomorrow same time."

Kelsie said, "Thanks, Mike. Will do."

When she walked back down the street she'd come to Mike's by, the teen gang kids turned away so as not to be seen staring at her or daring to whistle.

Thirty-Eight

Joshua Marshall felt acutely uncomfortable about Kelsie. He no longer worried over her volatile feelings from what had been taken from her in life, first her mother, then Angel Savannah. Nor did he worry entirely for her safety. With the investigation securely buckled up and Wheeler out of the picture, he worried about what she might do. Nobody, not even someone with all the steel in their system that Kelsie had, could last long without exploding.

He shared his worries with his wife over dinner soon after the general meeting called to resolve how to handle the mess caused by Kelsie killing Melissa Paulstein.

"So she explodes, Josh. Then what?"

"'Then what' is by going haywire. She not only blows her job at Treasury but a brilliant career ahead of her, with an enviable pension at its end. She's the kind who'll never let her doctor brother help support her in her old age. She's too in the habit of supporting him."

Elaine laughed, and came around to his

side of the table, and poured more wine into his almost empty glass. "You've really got it for this kid, haven't you."

"She's like having a daughter, Elaine, and you'll feel the same way when you meet her. You'll worry as much as I do about her maybe going off the deep end."

Elaine gave his shoulders a hug and went back to her seat before she said, "What's wrong with you, Josh?"

"What do you mean?"

"I mean, I'm married to a guy who usually gets off his butt and does something instead of just worrying about it."

Chiding from his wife almost always produced action on Joshua's part. He called his office the following morning after breakfast, said he wouldn't be in until after lunch, then got in his car and, braving Beltway traffic, headed into Washington and the Lincoln Park area. It took him a moment to find the right quiet street again, and then spot the house, but when he final did, he was lucky to find a parking space fairly close by. Leaving his car securely locked, he headed for the steps to the door.

Before he could set foot on them, he found his way blocked by a heavy-set man who, in spite of the summer weather, was wearing a disguising light coat that told Joshua he was carrying a gun, most likely in a shoulder holster. Remembering that Gareth was on witness protection, he flashed his Treasury badge, and when the man nodded and waved him on, went to the door, rang the bell, and waited. Very soon he heard someone inside coming, the door abruptly opened, and he found himself looking at Gareth.

Joshua said, "Good morning. Is your sister home?"

Gareth started to reply, got "My sister," then recognized Joshua. "Hey, you were here before. Looking for immigrants."

"That's right," Joshua said. "And told you I was ICE. Well, I wasn't." He produced his ID. "I'm Joshua Marshall. I work with Kelsie at FinCen."

Joshua's name wasn't unknown to Gareth. Kelsie had mentioned it several times. He said, "Gee, Mr. Marshall," and as he ushered Joshua into the living room, "She's not here. She went up to New York for some reason or other."

"New York? Did she say why? She's on rest leave, so we don't keep track."

"Hardly. My sister never tells me what she's up to. To me, most of her work life is a blank."

"She didn't tell you what she was doing in Connecticut?"

"Well, yeah. That job she told me about. And for the first time ever. And probably only because I caught her washing blood out of her shirt and jeans. Some guy came for her, she said, but got someone else by mistake. And then she shot somebody herself."

Surprised at his casualness, Joshua said, "Did she tell you who? I mean whom she shot?"

222

"No, she didn't. Well, somebody called Melissa, that's all, and I'm not sure I want to know. My sister killing someone? Kelsie? I can't believe it."

Joshua knew a cover-up when he saw one. He'd encountered more than his share when with the SPLC and had learned when to challenge and when not to. It was clear Kelsie must have told her brother a lot more than just shooting Melissa Paulstein and cautioned him not to talk under any circumstances to anyone about it.

Putting a closing smile on it, Joshua said, "You don't see that side of her at home?"

"Are you kidding? Nothing like. I mean I know she carries a gun. I've seen it. But with me it's 'Pick up your socks,' and 'Make your bed,' and 'It's your turn to wash the dishes,' and 'What would you like to have for dinner?' Mother stuff. Never stops. You'd think I was still back in middle school or something."

"Did she say when she'd be back from New York?"

"She didn't, but I know it has to be tomorrow sometime because she's going to a dinner at Number One Observatory Circle."

Joshua barely managed to hide his surprise. "The vice president's home?"

"Yeah."

"Did she say why?"

"No."

Again seeing cover-up discomfort in Gareth's expression, he felt he was treading dangerous waters, and decided to end his visit. He managed not to react, other than casually, and kept a straight face.

He said, "Okay, sounds like fun. Tell her I dropped by. Just to see how she was."

He thanked Gareth for his time, congratulated him on his graduating and on planning medical school, shook his hand, and left. But back in his car, he surrendered to a turmoil of anxious thoughts. Questions raced, one after another. Why on earth would she be going to a reception where the guests had to be mostly high-ranking officials in the Administration? How could she possibly have received an invitation? What on earth was she planning? How did she think to get by the VP-assigned Secret Service?

None of it made sense. Unless …? And then: Wait! Of course. New York, someone named Mike. A conversation he'd once had with Kelsie, long before she'd gone off to Europe to chase down the laundered Russian money, came back in jumbles. Mike lived in the world of Mafia gangsterism she'd penetrated when working for the Brooklyn DA. Some mid-level criminal she'd turned up innocent of a murder and saved from life or worse.

And that's why she'd gone to New York. He was sure of it. People in that Mafia world falsified documents and identification the way others sent Christmas or birthday cards. Could she have got herself an invitation, or even the right ID to penetrate the Secret Service? Okay, maybe, but it didn't say why, in the first place, she was going to the reception.

Darker thoughts began to crowd in. Everything he'd learned from the kindly old deacon. Kelsie being the VP's daughter. What the VP had done to her mother, then her surrogate mother, Angel Savannah, Black like himself and deeply loved. Cursing her out with the N-word in front of a young girl with a heart filled with grieving. A girl shattered and ever since torn within by a hatred she covered with icy coldness in a job that was as tough as it was merciless, and in itself more than a protective cover but a way to express those feelings that was not injurious to herself or her brother.

Was Kelsie Gordon planning to use the vice president's reception to expose his vileness to the whole world? Or worse? Joshua felt a tightness in his chest. She'd killed twice. Killing a third time might be easy.

Unknown to Joshua Marshall, Gareth Gordon was having the same thoughts.

Thirty-Nine

Kelsie made a pretense of being relaxed and without a care in the world. She sank deep into the couch, legs curled under, a drink in her hand, and pretended to watch TV. She was lying to Gareth and hated it. But felt she had to. She'd woken that morning deeply regretting she'd ever told him what she planned, every instant of it. Now the least she could do was to set his mind at rest, at least halfway, so perhaps he wouldn't spend the entire evening while she was at the reception wondering how it was going, imagining every word she spoke, their father spoke, fearful of every minute that would pass and in a state of acute anxiety until he thought it had ended, and then wondering how it had been. How had their father taken it?

Gareth said, "When do you leave?"

"I don't."

"You were going to the observatory, the reception for the vice president." He hated saying the very words *vice* and *president*. He had barely been holding on for hours, everything in him crawling with fear as the dread time for her to go came closer and closer. He'd barely got the words out.

"Changed my mind."

"Not going?"

"I don't have an invitation."

"I thought your job. I mean the Treasury Department and all that."

"I thought so too, but it turned out to be a no-no. Only VIPs and Administration officials are invited. Formal written letters, all that, and without one I'm sure the Secret Service would stop me the moment I showed."

Gareth stared at her, half incredulous. For twenty-four hours he'd forced himself to accept what she had said, to accept what she planned— to confront their father because she could no longer live with hiding from him. Now, in both belief and disbelief in what he'd just heard her say, he slowly began to give way to relief.

He said, hoping to hear with every word the answer he wanted to hear, "You're not going. That's definite?"

"I told you. I'd probably not be allowed near the place."

"Kels, you're sure? I mean you really have changed your mind."

"Sure, sure." For as long as she could remember, she had never deliberately lied to him. Had lectured him constantly about not lying to her whenever she or the therapist had had to pick up the pieces after he'd gone back on drugs. But she was going to do what she'd planned. Had to. Her mind was made up, and nothing would change it or stop her. She couldn't live any longer without doing it. Mike had said revenge got you nowhere. She'd heard that, and Mike was right. But she wasn't seeking revenge. Not any longer. She was simply doing what she had to do.

She ignored his disbelieving stare, but in the few moments of silence before she spoke again, she knew she was winning, became certain of it. Gareth believed her, trusted her. Because he always had, just as she had always believed and trusted him, except for when he was cheating on drugs. It made her feel sick, but she kept up the charade. And to reinforce what she saw, she made a point of casually switching TV channels from CNN to a hated sitcom.

"Don't worry about me," she said. "I'm fine. There's a movie I want to watch. You go on out. I know you've been dying to. Some basketball game? Do you have a date for it?"

It was finally good enough for Gareth. His personal desire overtook his slowly discarding fears and anxieties. Kelsie wasn't going, she'd be home all evening, he didn't have to cancel his date and the tickets he had for the game.

He said, "Well, okay. I'm going out, then."

"Got a date?"

"Yeah."

"Have fun." She hated saying it, hated her saying it to *him*. She hated that when he headed for the front door and said, "See ya," that he probably wouldn't. Or she him. She had no idea if either of them would ever see the other again, and her heart felt shattered by it. She had to struggle to keep from breaking down.

She waited a while to make certain Gareth wasn't coming back for some reason, tickets for the game or his date's address. Then she dumped her half-finished drink. She'd had enough to steel her resolve. She wouldn't, shouldn't, have more. She needed a completely clear head. More so than on any other job she'd been on, and this time it wasn't for the Treasury Department, nor for the DA in Brooklyn, but for herself and for Gareth.

She went upstirs, had a shower, washed her hair, spent some time with it wrapped in a towel as she sat at her dressing table doing her makeup. Satisfied she'd not put on too much, nor too little, she rose and got a dress from her closet, one she felt would be right for the reception. Doing so, she smiled wryly to herself. The last time she'd dressed properly had been at Soundview and the dinner for financial friends of Paulstein, among them viciously racist company presidents and CEO's hiding behind their titles and the theoretical respectability of their companies, white nationalists accepting Russian money to help them sow divisiveness throughout America.

Satisfied that she looked okay, she blow-dried her hair and put on the same costume jewelry she had worn that night at Paulstein's. How long ago had that been? A century or so at least.

And at a time before she had got onto Melissa's sick viciousness and the appalling double game she was performing, part of her obeying Wheeler, the other her own interests.

Satisfied she'd pass, at least where appearance was concerned, Kelsie went back downstairs and threw a light coat over her shoulders. Summer evenings were often cool, and it would help in her general disguise. Then, before she left, she removed her little Beretta Minx from her shoulder bag and tucked it carefully into her evening purse, along with the Secret Service ID she'd received from Toni Gambetta in Brooklyn, and with the immaculate letter of invitation he'd forged for her. Only the most experienced forensic eye, aided by modern technology, could have spotted that both were fakes, and one or the other would suffice, she thought.

There was one last thing she needed to do before she left. She went into the living room and took Angel's reframed photo from its place in the bookcase. "I'm on my way, Angel," she whispered. "Wish me luck." She kissed the photo gently, then put it back, turned out the lights, and left.

Forty

Kelsie took an Uber to Observatory Circle. Her own car remained where she'd parked it earlier that day, almost directly in front of her house, its keys with a brief note left on the living room cocktail table before the couch where she'd left everything else for Gareth.

The Uber had hardly crossed Rock Creek Park and left Massachusetts into Observatory Circle when it was stopped by uniformed Secret Service. The driver jerked his thumb toward the back seat, and Kelsie lowered her window in time to be half blinded by the guard's flashlight, shone directly at her face. She managed a smile and said, "I'm due at the reception."

The guard took a look at her clothes and grooming and decided she probably was. "You'll have to walk," he said. "No unofficial cars allowed."

"Not a problem." Kelsie thank her driver and got out of the car. The vice president's home didn't look all that far; its interior lights were blazing, and she could see a few couples on the terrace that half surrounded one side of the big

Victorian building.

"Can I see your ID, please."

Kelsie fumbled in her evening purse and got out her driver's license, along with a much folded letter on personal stationary, headed "From the Desk of Corinna Arthur," in Corinna's bold scrawling hand. It said how much she looked forward to seeing her at her father's reception, and hoped it wouldn't be all work for her, and that they'd get a chance to talk, and was signed "In haste and much love, Corinna." The officer briefly inspected both and then said, rather curtly, she thought, "You don't match our list of expected guests this evening, Miss Gordon."

Kelsie was ready for it. "I'm not surprised," she said brightly. "I'm last-minute. As you read, Miss Corinna expects me. You can check with her." She glanced up at the mansion and laughed. "That's if you can find her."

Secretly she held her breath, and managed not to let it out visibly when the guard, as she had gambled on, backed off and said, "Of course. Enjoy the evening, Miss Gordon."

But as she left him and started up the short distance to the mansion, she saw him get onto his cell, and intuitively she knew she wasn't free yet. There'd be more.

She was right. Virtually at the door, she was stopped by two agents in tuxedos. "Miss Gordon?"

She stopped and once again smiled brightly. "More ID? My invitation was checked by your colleague." She nodded toward the uniformed guard, now busy checking another late arrival.

"If you don't mind, Miss Gordon."

"Don't mind at all. I've been assigned to Miss Corinna."

"I beg your pardon? Assigned?" Both agents looked half startled, half puzzled.

Kelsie said, "You weren't told? I'm special unit. She's had some kind of problem and asked for someone to be close by her all evening who would seem to fit. We've been friends since school, and it's probably why I'm not on the guest list." She reached into her purse again and produced her fake Secret Service ID, along with the letter of invitation, and handed both to one of the agents. "I'm Kelsie Gordon, number 3723. I've really had to scramble to get here. You guys are lucky you don't have to go through what a girl does to get ready."

A flashlight shone, the ID and Corinna's letter were passed by one man to another and then back, and returned to Kelsie. "Caught us flat-footed, Kelsie. Enjoy whatever you're in for. Better you than me with Corinna." His companion laughed and said sarcastically, "Good luck, pal."

Kelsie joined his laughter with a knowing wink and went up the four steps to the porch, and under the broad canopy joining the terrace to her right, and then through the open front door, thanking heaven that she'd taken the precaution to get two fake IDs, the Secret Service identity as well as the letter of invitation. So far, so good.

Forty-One

Once inside the wide circular foyer, with its narrow stair leading to the floor above, to her relief she found far more people than she'd expected. She was prepared for possible recognition by her father, and that the place was crowded would help. Then there was the simple fact that he hadn't seen her for several years— nearly ten, to be exact. She counted that she would be so out of context that he would never in his wildest dreams expect her to be there.

Just the same, every part of her went into a tense defense mode, and for nearly half an hour, while never taking her eye off him, she drifted among couples as close to him as she dared, and trying to look like somebody who truly belonged.

Several times she politely shrugged off advances from men, some clearly married as well as unmarried ones, while all the time critically aware that she had to get her father by himself, and that she would have to be near enough to follow him especially if he left the room even for a minute. When that moment would come, she didn't know, except that she could only count on it happening.

Given his hosting and always being surrounded by well-wishers, his daughter Corrina ever close by, she was beginning to think she'd failed when that moment came, and quite unexpectedly. She saw her father excuse himself from several people he was talking to and abruptly slip his way, with smiles and nods, through the many guests when heading, she at first thought, for one of the two bathrooms on the mansion's north side, beyond the lounge. Instead he went straight up the stair.

Nobody seemed to be watching him, and taking a deep breath, she followed. Getting to the top, she didn't see him for an instant, and thought she had lost him, but then caught sight of him as he went through the open door of what appeared to her to be a small study, a place with comfortable chairs, a desk, and a wall lined with books. She followed quickly, and as he flicked on the lights, and before he could turn to shut the door, she was inside the room with him and had shut the door herself, and reaching behind her, locked it.

When, startled, he turned in blank surprise, she said, "You don't remember me, do you." And as surprised recognition did then began to lash his features, she said, "I'm your daughter, Kelsie. Remember? Or have you tried so hard to forget that you can't."

With an ugly sound, he stepped toward her, but he was too late. Kelsie's little Beretta, leveled straight at his face, stopped him. Fear replaced anger. He turned white and gasped.

Kelsie said quietly, "No, I'm not going to shoot you. Not yet, anyway, unless you force me to. Go over to the desk." She backed him slowly toward it until he stood by it, then, waving the Beretta at its chair, said coldly, "Sit down." When he did, she said, "I'm going to give you a chance you don't deserve, you rotten bastard."

She pulled from inside the front of her dress a carefully folded sheet of legal-size writing paper, unfolded it, and spread it on the desk in front of him. "Something for you to sign," she said. "It says that you acknowledge you are the father of Gareth Gordon by Andrea Gordon for whom you then bought a home in a deal to hide your adultery, and that you undertake your obligation to pay his college loan both from the American University and from whatever medical school he enters this fall."

She paused, allowing his terrified eyes to fall on the paper, then reached across the desk and pulled a pen from a fancy marble pen and pencil holder that had on its base the Seal of the Vice President of the United States. "Sign it," she said coldly. "Right away, and no arguments. If you don't, I'm going straight downstairs to announce to all your guests who I am, who Gareth is, and how for years you have failed to recognize our existence."

SHE WASN'T AWARE, NOR was the vice president,

that at that moment Joshua Marshall pulled his car to a skidding stop at the gates of the observatory. He leapt out, and without waiting to be challenged, thrust his Treasury identification in the startled face of the uniformed Secret Service man standing guard.

"Did a young woman come in here a few moments ago? Unescorted. Probably showed an ID?" Joshua didn't wait for an answer. He said, "Immediate red alert. Fast. Assassination attempt." He'd hardly stopped speaking when he was on the run, up the driveway to the mansion's front door.

IN THE VP's STUDY, the door firmly locked and silencing the noise of the party below, Kelsie, confident she had forced her father's hand, was caught off guard when he suddenly and with surprising violence pushed the chair back and leapt upright.

"You filthy little bitch," he shouted. "Who the hell do you think you're talking to? You have proof of nothing, and I'm not signing anything." He swung halfway around the desk and pushed close to her, livid. "I should have put you away years ago along with that black whore you called mother."

But then he stopped short, his face turning white again as he found himself staring directly into the dark round muzzle of the little Beretta, only a foot away and aimed directly between his eyes.

Gasping, he stepped back, but came up short against the desk, just as something in Kelsie snapped. She stepped close and shoved the muzzle of the gun into his gaping mouth. There was a rush of sound in her ears, drowning the terrible scream of her own voice. There was her father's sheet-white terrified face as all her grief and despair of years became everything: her mother's face gray with death in her coffin, Angel's crushed body in the street when she'd been run down.

One finger clicked off the little handgun's safety catch, and her trigger finger slipped through the trigger guard and around the trigger.

But there was no sound of a shot. There was only a sudden deathly silence. Her terrified father turning away, sinking slowly back into the desk chair. Her deadly little Beretta hanging from her finger by its trigger guard, and down by her side, before falling to the carpeted floor. Herself, sensing only a numbness that seemed to grasp her entire body. And with it a strange growing surprise that she hadn't pulled the trigger.

There'd been the Mafia hit man in the Bronx, there'd been Melissa Paulstein in Connecticut. Legal killings. Job killings. But now her father? What had stopped her? She didn't really know. Except it wasn't a job. It wasn't undercover defense, and she wasn't an undercover agent. This was her life with her brother, Gareth. She hadn't been able to pull the trigger, to kill again.

She had sat down opposite her father and

had just put the Beretta back in her evening purse when the Secret Service burst into the room.

She said quietly, as they seized her, "It's okay. My father has just had a rather upsetting surprise."

The cold hard truth of where she was and what she'd almost done swept in then. She'd come seeking justice for her brother, that Gareth be legally recognized. She'd come for that and hadn't succeeded. She'd come also meaning to shoot their father once he'd signed the paper she'd given him to sign, and she hadn't.

Now there'd be no help from parental recognition, college loans paid. There would be bleak days ahead and only struggle. And yet she felt a strange calm. She hadn't failed. The truth would now be pulled out of him, whatever his denials. Without killing, she had destroyed the man who had kept her and her brother in darkness for years, had crucified their mother, and had caused the murder of their beloved guardian. And with his parentage finally revealed, her years of burning hate were somehow extinguished.

As she was taken away, her wrists handcuffed behind her back, through the shocked silent crowd downstairs, she had a sense of relief she'd never expected. There was now no more living a lie. It would only be minutes before news of what had happened would be seized by the media, that the rigidly evangelical vice president had two illegitimate children he'd never publicly acknowledged in order to hide his adultery while he rose to prominence in his church and in government.

The investigation would be endless, but she thought she would be cleared when it all came out. Her birthright revealed as well as her father's treasonously plotting and arranging for Russian money to sow divisiveness, racism, and disloyalty. She had been on his trail for a year, her life threatened twice while she sought to bring him to justice. Marie Suarez would stand by her along with all of her team. Others would too, the FBI when the truth was revealed of what she'd done in finally bringing Emanuel Arthur to earth.

The past was over. There was a new unknown future, and oddly, she felt a surge of hope. Gareth wasn't going to get what she'd promised herself for him, but she thought he'd understand why not when he stopped being angry with her for deceiving him. And he'd cope. And so would she. She'd work at no matter what, and for no matter whom, and between the two of them they'd manage. They always had. For all their powerful father had done to try to crush them, they'd been taught how by a mother and a guardian angel, two women who were stronger.

End

About the Author

 David Osborn, for over sixty years a writer, lives in Connecticut with his wife, a once American and European ballerina, then renowned in international health policy. Their daughter, a PhD psychologist, practices in Sydney, Australia. Their lawyer son is an advocate for the welfare of animals worldwide.

Also by David Osborn

Novels and Screenwriting

Novels

The Glass Tower – Hodder & Stoughton
Open Season – The Dial Press
The French Decision – Doubleday
Love and Treason – New American Library
Heads – Bantam
Murder on Martha's Vineyard – Lynx
Murder on the Chesapeake – Simon & Schuster
Murder in the Napa Valley – Simon & Schuster
The Last Pope – Source Books
The Cape Cod Blue – Dagmar Miura
Alicia's Secret (young adult) – Dagmar Miura
A Cold Wind from the Andes – Dagmar Miura
The Head Hunters – Dagmar Miura
Looking Back: The Long Life of a Writer (a memoir)
Delta Red – Dagmar Miura
Eventide – Dagmar Miura
The Somersville Bodies – Dagmar Miura
Cold Case 369 – Dagmar Miura
The Lighthouse (a novella) – Dagmar Miura
The Saugatuck Conspiracy – Dagmar Miura

For Children

Jessica and the Crocodile Knight (a novel) – HarperCollins

Jessica and Her Adventures in Fairyland (collection of five novellas) – Dagmar Miura

Ophelia and Her Forest Friends (series of ten stories) – Dagmar Miura

Jessica and the Witch's Broom – Dagmar Miura

Jessica and the Flying Unicorns – Dagmar Miura

Jessica and the Golden Swan Feather – Dagmar Miura

Feature Films

The Trap (original story and screenplay; Academy Award nominee for Best Foreign Film) – Columbia

Open Season (screenplay, adapted from Osborn's own best-selling novel *Open Season*) – Columbia

Chase a Crooked Shadow (original story and screenplay co-written with Charles Sinclair; listed by the British Academy of Motion Picture Science as "One of the ten best suspense scripts ever written") – Warner Bros.

Moment of Danger, a.k.a. *Malaga* (screenplay adapted from the novel) – Warner Bros.

Malaga (screenplay) – Warner Bros.

Maroc 7 (original story and screenplay) – J. Arthur Rank

Deadlier Than the Male (original story and screenplay) – J. Arthur Rank

Some Girls Do (original story and screenplay) – J. Arthur Rank

The Road to Dusty Death (screenplay) – J. Arthur Rank

The Games (screenplay) – Associated British

Follow the Boys (original story and screenplay) – MGM

Beat Girl (original story and screenplay) – Renown Films/British Lion

Stop-over Forever (original story and screenplay) – British Lion

Winter Holiday (original story and screenplay) – MGM

Penny Gold (original story and screenplay) – J. Arthur Rank/Columbia

Whoever Slew Auntie Roo? (original story and screenplay) – Paramount & American International

Murder, She Said (screenplay, Agatha Christie adaptation) – MGM

Murder at the Gallop (screenplay, Agatha Christie adaptation) – MGM

Feature-length Documentaries

Fangio, The History of Formula One Racing (original screenplay; executive producer) – Volpi Productions

Why Ireland – Irish Tourist Bureau

Films Canceled While in Production

HMS Ulysses – Volpi Productions (screenplay adaptation of the Alistair MacLean novel about protecting North Sea convoys to Russia during World War II; production halted when a key warship was unavailable)

The Mad Motorists – Volpi Productions (screenplay adaptation from the Allen Andrews novel about the 1907 Peking to Paris race)

Eagle at Sundown – Dragon Films (original screen story about Napoleon's escape from Elba; starring Douglas Fairbanks; in production when canceled)

Les Petits Rats – Disney (original story and screenplay about the Paris Ballet school; production begun, then canceled)

Hunters' Horn – McCahon Productions (screenplay adaptation from the Harriette Simpson Arnow novel; production canceled; financing failure)

Blood on the Rose – British Lion (screenplay adaptation from the Phyllis Hastings novel)

Television

Bouquet for Miss Olive (three-act play; British Television Producers Association nominee for Best Play of the Year) – Granada/ITV

Three on a Gas Ring (three-act play; British Television Producers Association nominee for Best Play of the Year) – Granada/ITV

Why George Brown Hanged (three-act play) –
  Granada/ITV

Arthur of the Britons (pilot and three scripts on
  the life of King Arthur; Writers Guild of
  Great Britain award winner for Best British
  Children's Series)

The Antiquers (original story, pilot, and six
  episodes in the sitcom series) – Irish National
  Television